BLACKFISH
WHITE POINTER

BY
JOHN LEE SCHNEIDER

SEVERED PRESS
HOBART TASMANIA

BLACKFISH WHITE POINTER

"When you enter the ocean, you enter the food chain... and not necessarily at the top"

-Jacques Cousteau

CHAPTER 1

They called him Doby.

He was an old whale, and he was known up and down the Pacific as a kind of icon to the whale-watchers, who had given him his name.

His giant squared head, trademark of the sperm whale, was instantly recognizable for a lifetime of scars – battles with rivals, encounters with Japanese whalers – his hide was lashed and gouged by the tentacles and beaks of giant squid.

Now a massive bull in his prime, Doby stretched seventy-feet from nose to tail, and weighed more than sixty-five tons. He was the largest, most powerful predator on the planet – perhaps ever.

Today, he was prey.

This time, he was being chased by orcas.

If there was one axiom of the sea – if orcas wanted you, they *got* you.

Their common name was rumored to have come from an inversion of the Spanish translation 'whale-killer'.

In recent days, they had lived up to their name.

Doby had limited encounters with orcas throughout the majority of his travels. The transient-pods that hunted whales tended to go for smaller, easier targets, like minke whales, or even the larger, toothless baleens.

A big cachalot was another story, let alone Doby himself.

Big males like Doby tended to travel alone – living separate from the pods of females that congregated in the tropics, except when mating periodically brought them together.

Doby was unique among big dominant males. While he mated with multiple females from several pods each year, he tended to linger in the area. Some researchers had suggested he was simply the biggest, *most* dominant bull, and his extended stay was a way of saying so.

Others, however, had noted that he was one of those odd males – particularly rare among large *old* males – that would join up with a pod for a time, before making his solitary way back north, to the colder, richer feeding grounds necessary to support his massive bulk.

Each year, Doby always returned in the company of the same pod – the same senior female, along with her sisters and calves. Since records had been kept, this had been a consistent pattern for twenty years, and possibly long before that. They stayed together until they reached the deep canyons off southern California, before parting ways, and Doby would continue north for the season.

Whale watchers called the big female 'Berta'. They also nicknamed her 'Doby's Girl'.

Doby didn't measure time the way people do, nor did he know the human name they had given the big female – only that she had been his very first mate, and he had known her for as long as he could remember.

The orcas had taken her yesterday.

It had been a three-hour ordeal.

Doby had never seen the likes of it before. In his few clashes with orcas, he'd always managed to chase off any cheeky enough to press too close to him, or any of his mating females.

But these orcas had been relentless. In the past week, they had taken both calves – his own offspring from previous years – along with the other young adult female that had comprised Berta's pod.

Then they had taken Berta herself.

Doby had battled back as best he could. Until now, his size and strength had always been enough. But this time, the smaller, faster orcas had corralled him, harassed him, never quite in range of either his teeth or mighty tail, as they took turns ramming and bludgeoning. They first went for the smaller infants, forcing them below the surface and drowning them, before moving in to separate the larger cows.

Berta fought ferociously, first for her calves, and then for her sister. But in the end, she had succumbed as well, battered, torn, and drowned.

Doby had stumbled on to her remains just an hour ago – left floating lifelessly, her tongue stripped-out, as was the way with orcas – with the remainder of the carcass simply discarded, seemingly to waste.

Of course, nothing really goes to waste in the ocean. What orcas left behind was bounty for sharks, arriving in packs to gorge opportunistically. Probably ninety percent of the whales killed by orcas, along the Pacific migration routes, were consumed by sharks.

And there were a lot of sharks lately.

Off this stretch of southern California, these were big, mature Great Whites, traveling their own migratory paths, diverting their attention from the normal pit-stop seal colonies dotting the coast, to the orca-sponsored smorgasbord of meat and blubber, growing full and fat on free protein.

Doby found them suckling at Berta's carcass like piglets on a sow.

Sperm whales – *Physeter macrocephalus* – the '*cachalot*' – were known as some of the more intelligent of whales, especially among large cetaceans.

Perhaps it is not anthropomorphism, but simple common experience, to suggest that Doby grieved.

And perhaps, at the sight of the scavenging Great Whites, he even felt a pulse of anger.

Doby lurched forward, scattering the sharks, and he had stayed in the area in the time since, as if guarding the carcass.

Then he had detected that first, tell-tale ping, echoing stealthily through the water.

A sonar-blip. A communicating orca.

They had taken his family, and now they were after him.

Death had been in the air for weeks, now.

As he had made his way down the coast this season, he had encountered multiple slaughtered carcasses – far beyond need. In the way that sea creatures understood things, Doby had sensed something badly dysfunctional.

He had been hearing it all over the ocean – notably, in the odd sounds coming from the normal migrating pods of transient orcas.

None of these so-called 'whale killers' had ever bothered him, and certainly not in a year when smaller **minke whales** and other easier prey were so bountiful.

But this year, the echoing blips from these ocean-going orcas carried a note of discord.

There were similar emanations from the traveling pods of baleens – a general sense of wrongness – which, in baleens, often caused them to panic and beach themselves. Doby had seen entire pods of his larger, brill-toothed cousins, littered along the coast, suffocated by the weight of their own mass pressing down on their lungs.

Of course, a cachalot was made of sterner stuff – Doby wasn't going to beach himself just because a bunch of orcas started spouting. He would fight.

Just as he had when they took each of the others.

He would fight as they killed him too.

And as suddenly as that, out of nowhere, they were upon him.

He had just come to the surface for a breath, when they hit him from both sides, skimming just under the surface and swimming sideways to hide their dorsal fins, they rammed into his ribs.

Doby was a powerful animal, easily a physical match for any orca, but his smaller cousins worked in tandem, and some of them weighed-in at a respectable five tons or better, themselves, charging in at thirty-five knots. Mass-times-velocity-equals-power, and the air was cruelly blasted from his lungs.

Before he even began to react, he was hit again, this time from below, directly into his gut – an impact that nearly caused him to suck water.

Doby began to thrash as the harlequin shapes circled, dolphin-like, just out of range. Next, they would start biting at his fins, like wolves going for the ankles of moose.

The big cachalot surged for the surface, desperate for another breath. If he could sound, he could take them deep – not even an orca could follow a sperm whale all the way to the bottom. But while he tarried at the surface, he was vulnerable from below.

As if on cue, he was struck another terrific impact, dead in the chest. And suddenly there were two orcas beside him, pushing him back down before he could take air.

A few more blows underwater and they would drown him.

Doby thrashed wildly, and the orcas quickly gave ground, fading back out of reach.

His spout blasted as he finally took a deep, sucking breath.

Regrouping, the orcas circled at distance. Doby now got his first good look at them.

He had long been aware that there was something different about these orcas. They were not the normal migrating pods. At least one of the old males had a drooping fin.

Then there was their bizarre dialect, that seemed to mix elements of widely diverse orca eco-types – kind of a hodgepodge jail-talk.

Doby didn't think about these things, so much as he perceived them. More importantly, he recognized that, for whatever reason, this rogue pod was an immediate threat to his life. And fighting back wasn't going to be enough.

He took his breath and prepared to retreat, perhaps for the first time in his mature life, fleeing like a common bait-fish.

But even as he did so, the first of them darted in – a big female, recognizable by the smaller, hooked fin – and she grabbed Doby's tail-fluke in her jaws, cleaving off three solid feet. At nearly the same moment, a big male clamped onto his pectoral fin.

Doby rolled, twisting his mass into a downward corkscrew, preparing to dive deep.

He was hit again in the gut, right between the ribs. He kept his breath – barely – but he was momentarily stunned.

Around him, the black-and-white shadows started to circle in.

Doby gathered himself, preparing to fight to the last.

And then, abruptly, the assault ceased.

The ocean around him was suddenly empty.

Doby floated for a moment, regaining his senses.

Then he became aware of an approaching drone.

It was a boat motor – Doby had learned caution around the sound. Apparently, the orcas had too.

Doby let himself drift, fading into the darker deep, his wounds clouding the surrounding water with his blood.

On the surface, a small boat pulled next to Berta's floating carcass.

For the moment, the sharks had not yet dared return.

Humans, on the other hand...

One of the men leaned over and threw a boat-hook into Berta's hide. He pulled the floating blubber closer to the boat.

"Hey, Pete," he said, "this look like orca to you?"

The other man leaned over, running his hands along the torn lower jaw.

"Yeah," he sighed. "Looks like it."

"Think it's them?"

Pete didn't answer. He ran his hand over one of the shark-bites, which were all pretty damn big. And there were a *lot* of them. But they were all postmortem, and common on all whale carcasses at sea.

More significant was the torn jaw and missing tongue.

"Yeah," he said finally, "I think it's them."

Then he had frowned, looking uncomfortably at the surrounding water.

"But I also think that's not the only thing that's wrong around here."

And not a hundred feet below, Doby circled, looking up at the shadow hovering above, one more suckling piglet at Berta's carcass – not much different than a shark, from his vantage.

For a moment, Doby felt a moment of impulsive rage. He actually flicked his flukes, and turned for a split-second towards the surface.

But even as he did so, the movements caused him pain. He had been pummeled brutally. His tail and fin were torn and bleeding.

He also found himself recalling a few hairy incidents with whalers and harpoon-cannons, and knew humans were not to be underestimated.

Doby did not recognize pride, as a person would understand it. He only knew that he was hurting, and remembering old scars – and his nerve now failed him.

He was not like a man, who might curse himself a coward. He was simply an animal, injured and frightened – humbled for perhaps the first time in his life.

He fled for the depths, diving deep.

But he remembered.

CHAPTER 2

"Stay frosty, guys," Quinton said, "there's sharks."

There was a static buzz in his headset, and he looked to the other members of his Coast Guard dive-team, making sure they got the message. They all waved, nodding their heads, blowing bubbles, and making motions to look over their shoulders.

"There's been orcas in the area," Hendricks responded. "That'll scare off any sharks."

"You *hope*," Gardner answered, and there was a generalized chuckle.

Quinton was happy to note, however, that they all kept one dutiful eye to their backs as they floated above the wreck.

"Wow," Hendricks said, "that's a mess."

They were getting their first clear look at what was definitely a less-than-routine salvage.

Lieutenant Quinton Shaw had been in the Guard for twenty years, and the aftermath of every wreck always told its own story.

They were currently perched just at the point where the coastal shelf dropped off into deep ocean, less than a mile from shore. The surrounding water was moody-gray and indistinct.

Quinton was feeling uncharacteristically nervous.

He had dived in these waters all his life, and he had salvaged many boats, both as a Guard officer, and before that, a Navy SEAL. He had also seen his share of human wreckage.

Some were harder than others. Sometimes you knew them.

This had already been the worst in a long-string of bad shark-years, but today had been one of the most violent incidents Quinton had ever seen. At least four fatalities.

It had been going on at Surf Shore for a long time – nearly a decade. This season wasn't halfway over, and Quinton was already weary of death – it befouled the air.

Once a popular resort-spot, Surf Shore had been plagued by repeated attacks over the last eight years.

Eerily, they struck like clockwork, every two seasons – always off the same beach, always the same time of year, once even on the exact same day, two years apart. Those mindful of the ways of Great Whites, knew that this also happened to coincide with the migratory patterns of the big females.

Going into this year, the tally had been five surfers hit, four fatally – two kayaks, both survived.

And then earlier this season, just a few short weeks ago, one boat. Another fatal incident, falling right into the two-year pattern.

The young lady who had been taken, was someone Quinton had known well – an adventurous young activist, who had foolishly placed herself out on rough ocean around a troupe of large Great Whites scavenging a whale carcass.

One of them had apparently taken a bite out of her *fourteen-foot* boat and sunk her right there among the feeding sharks. She was never found.

That was the part that bothered Quinton the most – the thought of what remained of her, left down here alone.

Quinton had known Carson Sheridan since she was a teenager, an ocean-going beauty, who lived on adrenaline, with a reputation for reckless stunts – Quinton had once caught her out past the shipping lanes after midnight with a boatload of drunken sorority sisters. It was hard not to admire that sort of sheer pluck and utter fearlessness, especially combined with her pure and honest love for the ocean.

Although, it was possible that love was a little *too* genuine – perhaps even fostering a belief it was a love returned.

Carson was particularly famous for free-swimming with BIG sharks – including an on-camera swim with an estimated twenty-foot Great White – in a thong-bikini, no-less.

That one had drawn wide criticism from the more-serious science community, but the video had gone viral, and actually inspired an entire series – *Sharks and Babes*, starring her and a few bikini-laden friends.

Carson invoked a daredevil courage that seemed to make her immune to the obvious dangers that she exposed herself – like a mountain goat, casually dancing over cliffs, defying death as a matter of happenstance, with every step.

Until just that last time.

The local community had been shaken – not only was Carson well-liked, it was an illusion shattered.

It had also, unfortunately, led to the mess Quinton was here to clean-up today.

The press had latched on to Surf Shore's 'two-year killer-shark' myth, and when the season did indeed claim another victim – and not *just* a victim, but a well-known *shark*-activist – a local news-producer had chartered a boat out to the same damned waters.

In the manner of pure, brazen fools, they had teased-up another group of feeding Great Whites – *and* decided to go for-crissake-*cage*-diving.

They thought it would make great TV.

What could possibly go wrong?

The results of *that* little ill-advised foray lay on the ocean floor before them.

That brought the tally to *two* boats, this year, taken down by large sharks.

Today's incident had also very-nearly taken the life of yet another young lady of Quinton's acquaintance – Carson Sheridan's most-common partner in crime – on-line, she was known as the *other* blond in *Sharks and Babes*.

Lauren – *Doctor* Palmer, these days – was theoretically the careful one, yet there she was, on camera, in a thong. And she had been on-board the charter boat as 'scientific adviser'.

She was currently hospitalized, and damned lucky to be.

Quinton, who was a bit prideful, would clench his teeth and count his blessings, for Carson's semi-estranged, hooligan of an ex-boyfriend – a surf bum, named Cody, who Quinton had *long* disapproved of, but who also happened to *be* there – or else Lauren would have certainly died, along with everybody else on that charter.

It was exactly the sort of thing that happened when people disrespected the ocean.

The boat had overturned as it sank, and it now lay face-down on the bottom – a pose of submission.

The bite marks along the stern were disturbingly descriptive. They had gotten those sharks so teased-up, one of them swam up and bit the boat on the ass.

Again, biting boats was something Great Whites were prone to do, not necessarily for the people on-board, but because a boat was a big floating object in the water, like a whale carcass.

But this particular shark – a big, aggressive female, Carson and Lauren had nicknamed 'Big Rhonda' – happened to hit the engine compartment, punching a hole in the stern, dumping them into the schooling sharks.

Lauren had been caught in the cabin, as the boat sank seventy-feet, straight to the floor of the ocean shelf, less than a dozen yards before the drop-off – leaving her trapped, with a tiny air-tank, and surrounded by schooling sharks.

Cody was a text-message away, in his own boat, and from what Quinton had been told, the damned fool had *free-dived* straight through the middle of the frenzy. Armed with a powerhead, no less.

Quinton tried to imagine.

He hadn't yet gotten all the details, but the kid evidently pulled it off.

Shaw had done the math. By the time he and his Coast Guard team had arrived, Lauren's air would have run out.

Damn fool or not, Cody had made the difference.

When they caught-up back on shore, Quinton would make a point of telling him so.

It was ironic – when Carson had been alive, Cody and Lauren *hated* each other.

Minus Lauren, the death toll on the charter boat had been the ship's captain, the mate, and both reporters. No remains had yet been found.

Since this morning, Surf Shore's shark related fatalities had nearly doubled, up to nine.

By Quinton's measure, having been dumped into the middle of a feeding frenzy around a whale carcass, they couldn't even fairly said to have been *attacked* so much as simply *eaten*.

For shark-attack, old-time shipwrecks were the *real* horror shows – maritime disasters, that left entire crews of sailors as bait for packs of marauding sharks. Historically, the most prolific killer of humans would *have* to be the oceanic white-tip – an aggressive seafaring relative of tiger and bull sharks, who were always the first on the scene of wrecks.

That sort of thing rarely happened these days. To be hit by a shark at all was beating sweepstakes odds.

On the other hand, part of being a shark-victim was *being* there. In terms of the general population, the average human being's chance of being in a heavily Great White-infested area was pretty low – but if you *were*...

Well, then you were kind of beating the odds to avoid it, weren't you?

And, of course, within every population, there were animals that were more aggressive than others. Big Rhonda was case in point.

Lauren and Carson had been cataloging Great Whites in the area for years, and they all had names and personalities – all on camera, all with profiles on *Sharks and Babes*' website.

There was Mack the Knife, a seventeen-foot male, also known as Mack the Mako, for his mako-like twisting breaches. There was Jabberjaw, another big male, most often seen gorging at whale carcasses.

And of course, there was Bloody Mary, yet another gigantic female, every bit the size of Big Rhonda, but older, scarred, and much more subtle – so named because she was known to sneak up from behind – just like the woman in the mirror.

It had, in fact, been Bloody Mary with whom Carson had done her infamous free-swim, hanging lightly from Mary's dorsal, appearing no larger than a seal pup next to the five-thousand pound fish, as it cruised serenely, seemingly oblivious to the human remora clinging to her fin.

So... there *were* a lot of sharks out there. A lot of big mature adults.

But out of all of them, Rhonda had been far and away the most dominant and aggressive.

And while they couldn't conclusively finger Rhonda for all of the attacks over the previous eight years, she was known to be in the area on each occasion – and without a doubt, she had been responsible for sinking both boats.

In addition to that, she had *also* apparently been going after whales.

And not *just* whales. It seemed Rhonda had actually attacked and killed an orca calf – something Quinton had never heard of before.

That one had come back on her. Orcas didn't play that shit, and the calf's mother had responded in kind.

It had been a short fight.

White sharks didn't really have much of a chance against orcas, particularly when the whales were acting in groups. In recent years, there were numerous documented cases of killer whales predating on Great Whites. There was a famous incident in the Farallon Islands, only a few short miles up the coast, where an orca killed a white shark on camera – quite effortlessly, in fact, simply flipping the big shark onto its back, inducing tonic paralysis, and holding it there until it drowned.

But even more than the attack on the one shark itself, the sheer dominance of the orcas was conclusively demonstrated in subsequent weeks, as the entire population of Great Whites abruptly vacated the Farallons, ceding the entire area.

Experts at the time had been astounded, because the seals that congregated in those islands were an important seasonal food source for the sharks.

But there were numerous other cases worldwide. A population of South African Great Whites similarly vanished after being targeted by prowling orcas. The sharks' solution to orca-encroachment was quite simple – they got the hell outta Dodge.

Which made Rhonda's behavior all the more remarkable. She'd *killed* one of them.

Quinton was actually rather bothered at the thought. Such aberrant, out-of-character behavior in animals was always a cause for concern, let alone in a two-and-a-half-ton apex predator.

On the other hand, it might not be aberrant, so much as a natural response to the conditions that had developed in the region.

Lauren, as in *Doctor* Palmer, speaking on behalf of the oceanographic Institute that operated north of Surf Shore, had informed the Coast Guard just last week that the waters around Surf Shore had become dangerous for a reason.

As it turned out, only a few miles south of one of the primary surf-beaches, there was a new elephant-seal colony no one had known about. Pinnipeds, protected by law for decades, were currently enjoying a boom population, which necessitated more floor space, and they had found themselves a nice little cubby hole, in a modest cove, right near the drop-off.

This seal colony had accordingly attracted the sharks, who now had a second food-stop on their way to the Farallons.

As Lauren explained, that meant the white shark population in the area was at least a third greater than they had believed – *and* that this resort community bordered on Great White feeding grounds.

That would certainly explain Rhonda's seemingly unusual aggression. She was a big, dominant animal. In areas of highly-congested populations, it wasn't unusual for an alpha to act out.

That, combined with the presence of orcas, had obviously left Big Rhonda on edge. Animals will often attack in fear, or at the perception of a threat.

They were also known to be territorial.

Or, Quinton supposed, it was possible Rhonda had just decided she'd gotten big enough to take on an orca.

Her jaws worked wherever they were tried.

And Rhonda wasn't the only would-be alpha out there. Besides twenty-footers like herself and Bloody Mary, there were any number of other big females approaching eighteen and nineteen feet.

Like the seals they preyed upon, Great Whites were beneficiaries of protection laws, and the sharks had been given time to grow, both in size and population. As prey grew bountiful, the predators became well-fed, plentiful and fat.

That meant a lot of big sharks. A lot more than previously believed. That made these dangerous waters.

And while the last eight years might have already conclusively proved that, they now knew *why*.

But at least Rhonda herself was gone. And with her, Quinton at least believed the primary problem animal had been culled out.

As it turned out, he was wrong.

CHAPTER 3

The great fish did not know it was a star.

Bloody Mary had no idea she was the subject of a video series that had circulated world-wide – that there were, in fact, websites that bore her name, along with photos of her fin – always with snapshots of the bikini-laden maidens, who always seemed to be barging in on her water.

There were even memes going around – a still-shot of Mary behind Carson Sheridan's silhouette in the water, with the caption: 'She always appears from behind'.

Mary had never been measured, but most estimates put her at twenty-feet or better, and she was one of the largest Great Whites ever filmed in open ocean.

Bloody Mary and Big Rhonda were known to habitually follow the same migratory paths, and hunt in the same waters.

Mary's name had actually been brought up as a potential suspect in the chronic shark attacks that had plagued Surf Shore. She was, after all, certainly in the correct size range, and she had been stalking this stretch of coast for years. She was also a cagey hunter, never known to fall for the decoys photographers sometimes trailed behind boats, hoping to lure the sharks into spectacular breaches – but she never missed a seal.

She was also always the first on-hand whenever Big Rhonda hit something big enough to share – a very opportunistic freeloader.

Experts had argued for years whether the shark incidents off Surf Shore had been the work of one shark – or predominantly one shark – or if it was a simple matter of an increasing population.

The discovery of the new elephant seal colony and sudden jump in the realistic estimate of the local population had reignited that debate all over again.

None of that mattered to Mary, although, in the way that she remembered things, she retained the answers to all those questions in the rudimentary storage of her primitive brain.

Of the eight attacks on humans in previous years, five of them fatal, Mary had been responsible for all but one of them – the surfer who had lived.

Mary was known by researchers as a shark who didn't miss.

And while it had indeed been Big Rhonda who had struck Carson Sheridan's boat, it had actually been the opportunistic Bloody Mary, sidling in from behind, who had snatched Carson up as she struggled in the water, all while Rhonda circled her 'kill' in adrenalized posturing.

Mary had remembered the free-swim. She knew what the splashing creature in the water was. It was a prey-item – last time, it had been hanging on her dorsal, but now it was within reach.

It had also been Rhonda who hit the charter boat. Mary herself hadn't even really participated in the dog-pile – or dog-*fish* pile – as the kicking hominids had been dumped into the water. Truth to tell, there wasn't that much meat on them to fight for. Let the little dogs burn their energy.

But now, Mary was hungry. She had actually been quite spoiled, living along Big Rhonda's hunting route. She had gotten used to all those free calories, scavenging off of Rhonda's kills – patient enough not to engage Rhonda directly, but big enough to get more than her share before any of the others dared approach. Mary had pigged-out quite decadently on Rhonda's gray whale calf.

She had been of a similar mind when Rhonda had hit the little orca. However, on that particular occasion, she had hung unobtrusively down below, even as the rest of the pack surged forward to freeload.

Mary was a cagey old female, and there was perhaps a part of her prehistoric consciousness that recognized the larger implications of what Rhonda had done.

Grown to her current size, that meant a lot of cross-ocean trips, and experience bred wisdom, even in a fish.

Bloody Mary knew her way around orcas.

She avoided but knew not to be bothered by the whale hunters. And she made sure the shark-hunting off-shore pods never even saw her, because when she traveled the open ocean, she hovered near the bottom.

A shark's perceptions were not the same as a whale's, but each of the two recognized pertinent signals in the other's sounds and behaviors.

They each recognized the other as rivals, but it was usually a very one-sided affair.

But Bloody Mary was a sly one.

Over the years, she had taken an orca or two.

For whatever reason, Mary was perhaps just a bit more savvy than your average shark – and while she instinctively perceived orcas as threats and competitors, she also understood that they were potential prey.

Great Whites have been demonstrated to adapt their hunting tactics to different circumstances. Sharks who breach on one coast, will chase down seals underwater just a few miles north. Vertical 'Polaris' attacks, so often filmed from the surface, were sometimes acted out two-hundred feet below, in clear water where the shark's coloring made them invisible at a deeper depth.

Through instinct or terrorism, Mary had learned the way to hit a stronger enemy was by targeting the young. On her bi-annual jaunt across the open ocean, Mary had been known to hit the odd orca calf, and then retreat deep, sometimes for days, as the outraged mother refused to abandon the body, the sounds of her mourning echoing off the deep ocean canyons.

But eventually they always moved on. And Mary would rise up and feed on the abandoned calf.

Hit and run. Guerrilla tactics were Bloody Mary's specialty.

Rhonda's mistake had been going above the sight-line.

It hadn't been her fault, any more than Mary's approach had been to her credit. It was not a conscious decision – Rhonda was simply responding to whatever extra-tick of pugnacious aggression nature had programmed into her.

Mary had always stayed low, which Rhonda would have perceived as submission.

But it also, if need be, exposed Rhonda's vulnerable throat and belly.

And in regards to catching dinner, it let Rhonda do all the work.

Rhonda almost never saw Mary sidling up beside her, next to a dead elephant seal, slipping up from behind to take a huge, gluttonous mouthful of free dinner.

But Rhonda was gone now.

And Mary the freeloading scavenger up-shifted into active hunter. She settled into an easy drifting cruise, hovering just at that sweet-spot in the misty, filtered light.

There was still activity around the sunken boat, more of those odd little hominids that sometimes rode the waves on little boards across her feeding grounds.

They were a bit scrawny, a bit bony.

But she was hungry, and they were handy.

Bloody Mary could see them, shining their little lights hovering over the wreck, even as she circled in, edging ever closer – just like the lady in the mirror, drifting in from behind.

Lieutenant Quinton Shaw never saw her coming.

CHAPTER 4

It was after visiting hours, but Lauren was still awake when Lieutenant Hendricks arrived at the hospital, looking solemn.

Lauren's family and friends had long-since gone home. She was up watching the news and was surprised to find her own name was so-far absent.

They showed aerial footage of the wreck-site from that afternoon, still daylight – which as far as anyone could see, simply meant a chopper-view of several Coast Guard boats anchored over where the charter vessel had sunk.

Lauren herself suffered modest injuries. In the adrenaline of the moment, she hadn't even realized she'd broken a wrist. She had also lost most of a fingernail, along with assorted cuts and bruises all over her chest, shoulders and stomach, courtesy of the sharp rocky bottom, as she had wriggled herself free of the upturned boat.

More than anything, she was suffering just a bit of emotional shock. She hadn't noticed her cracked wrist, because she'd just seen a man bitten in half right before her eyes.

Rationally, Lauren recognized she indeed probably required first-aid, but an overnight hospital stay probably wasn't necessary.

Then everyone started showing up – her father, who *hated* all her 'shark bullshit' – her weeping mother, and all her friends – especially so soon after Carson's funeral.

Lauren had bawled. And she just wanted to be babied for a while.

The only off-note was Cody, who she'd last seen when the emergency vehicles and police met them at the docks, and he remained absent among well wishers.

Granted, as Carson's ex, he wasn't popular in *this* crowd, but all things considered, Lauren thought he might at least merit a good word in front of her own father.

She hadn't yet spared the details of her rescue – she'd actually been waiting to lay it on them, once Cody himself showed. It was the least she could do. She hadn't exactly been his friend when he and Carson were together.

But Cody had yet to make an appearance, and her father crunched his face when Lauren mentioned his name.

Probably, it was best to just let Cody be. It wasn't as if he hadn't already done her any favors today, not to mention that his last contact with Carson's family had earned him a night in jail.

Lauren still had the snapshot Carson had sent her, about three weeks after her tumultuous, year-long affair with Cody had battled its way to an inevitable conclusion. Cody had apparently dropped by, in an attempt at reconciliation, by unfortunate confluence, the same day Carson's former self-proclaimed *fiancé* – a med-student whose name Lauren could never remember, and who Carson had unceremoniously dumped when she and Cody had first met – had chosen to try and make his own move.

The picture Carson sent was med-student (or was it pre-med?), sporting a swelled and bandaged nose, and two dark puffy, nearly-shut black eyes. The message read, 'Cody stopped by today.'

Cody had been arrested, and forever condemned by Carson's parents, who *loved* med-students, and were not at *all* fond of surf-bums.

So that was why Lauren's father had rolled his eyes when she mentioned his name.

"Not *that* guy."

Still, Lauren would have expected at least a text.

She brightened when she saw Lieutenant Hendricks at her door. At first, she attributed the look on his face to concern for herself – and to an extent, it was.

On TV, the news-anchor was a painfully chirpy cover-girl, who managed to say her own name a lot – "I'm *Lacey* Chase" – and whose grim expression and overly-correct enunciation was like watching a seventies retro-mercial.

"Breaking news," the cover-girl said, "among the dead of an apparent shark attack on a charter boat, is our own reporter/producer, David Templeton. Details are pending as the official investigation continues, but this afternoon's incident is just the latest in a string of fatal shark attacks that have haunted this area of coast for years."

Lauren sat up to greet Hendricks as he removed his hat, smiling at her gently.

"Hey, girl," he said. "How are you doing?"

Lauren smiled, nodding at the television.

"They haven't mentioned me," she said.

Hendricks looked uncomfortable.

"They don't know about you yet," he said. He cleared his voice. "There's a couple things we haven't told them."

But he paused as Carson's picture flashed on-screen.

"Just two weeks ago," Lacey Chase continued, "local activist, Carson Sheridan's boat was attacked and sunk, in these very waters, by what experts conclude was a very large Great White shark. Her body was never found. Today's incident highlights the increasing danger from sharks in what was once a popular surfing community."

The cover-girl tossed her locks, curls bouncing like a shampoo-ad, her eyes serious as a schoolmarm.

"Some researchers have attributed this long-running series of attacks along this small stretch of beach, as attributable to a single large individual traveling along a migratory route. The so-called *rogue* shark."

Lauren rolled her eyes. That *wasn't* the 'rogue shark' theory.

"Others, however," Lacey Chase intoned, "have suggested these incidents are not the work of one animal, but due to an exploding population."

Lauren groaned. Sensationalist twit.

The screen shifted to outside Lauren's own office, back at the Institute, where her dedicated-to-the-point-of-annoying assistant, Nancy, was standing-in. Looking flustered, Nancy fielded questions in desperately serious monotone, a perfect complement to the cover-girl's solemn narration.

Lauren turned the sound down.

"Sorry," she said, turning her attention to Hendricks. "I know all that."

She started to smile, the long-suffering patient reassuring the concerned friend, but Hendricks' face remained grim.

"Listen," he said. "We've gotta talk." He nodded at the mute screen, shaking his head, and now Lauren saw the deep circles under his eyes.

"Len?" she said, suddenly frightened. "Is something wrong?"

"They haven't reported this yet," Hendricks said, "but we were working on the salvage. And Quinton.... the sharks weren't gone yet."

Lauren stared back for a solid heartbeat, blinking, disbelieving.

"I saw it hit him," Hendricks said. "It was *big*. It came out of nowhere. And it... took him."

Hendricks' own voice broke for just a moment. Quinton had been his friend for years.

Lauren felt the sting of tears – coming slowly, this time – she was already utterly, emotionally wrecked.

She had screamed today, and she had bawled. Now she just sobbed in helpless chokes as this wretched new reality sunk in.

Hendricks lay an uncertain hand on her shoulder.

"I'm sorry to tell you this, Lauren. I didn't want you to see it on the news. We're holding off until we find his ex-wife."

Lauren squeezed his hand.

"Listen," he said, "I gotta go. I had to flash my badge to get in here. But..." He stopped. "You gonna be alright?"

Lauren wiped her eyes. Sitting there alone, she now found herself wishing she was home.

"I'll be fine, Lenny," she said. "Thank you."

Hendricks glanced at the silent screen and the aerial view of the Coast Guard clean-up.

"Night, girl," he said, and shut the door behind him.

Lauren lay back, shutting off the TV. There was nothing there she wanted to see.

After a moment, she turned off the light above her bed.

Right now, she felt very alone.

Her phone blinked on her desk – no new messages. Cody still hadn't called. She actually found herself a little hurt.

Lauren lay in the dark for a long time, waiting for sleep to come.

CHAPTER 5

Bloody Mary was agitated.

Her posture was arched, fins prominent, as she cruised the coast – an animal primed for a fight.

Mary had long been a dominant animal in the region, but she'd mostly left dealing with upstarts to Rhonda – who was happy to oblige, having once bitten an uppity young fourteen-foot male nearly in half.

That was another video that had gone viral once the dead male's carcass had been recovered by fishermen.

But Rhonda was gone now. That meant Mary had to do some of her own muscle work.

There had been another windfall of dead whale meat – multiple carcasses this time. With the nasty taste of Quinton Shaw's rubber wet-suit still on her teeth, she and nearly every other shark in the area had gorged on sperm whale for nearly two days.

The feast had taken them in close to shore as the carcasses finally beached themselves, there to be found by early-morning beach combers – found covered with bites – BIG bites – and a lot *of* them.

They had banqueted on four whales just in the last week – two of them full-grown adults. That had been a lot of food.

But there had also been a lot of sharks – big, aggressive, in close-contact, with both sexes – the entire area was practically rank, charged with egos and hormones.

Mary could just *smell* it.

And in the background, even as the mob of them swarmed like hyenas upon their latest decadent free meal, they were all aware of the continued presence of orcas.

In years past, when the orcas had come to the Farallons, the white sharks had fled. They had done so again this year.

But this time, the orcas had followed.

When an animal who operates on instinct, fine-tuned over millions of years, encounters a scenario outside its experience, its behavior becomes unpredictable.

Among the oldest animals in the sea, as well as some of the longest living, sharks – and white sharks, in particular – were as in tune with the subtleties of the ocean and the ecosystem as any creature.

Mary could hear, for example, the sonar blips of cachalots.

When a whale screams, the noise carries. Over the last several days, Mary had heard the echoing cries, first of the infants, and then, the louder, baritone cries of their mothers

Likewise, she could hear the answering calls from all across the ocean. There were pods of baleens, shifting generations-old migrational patterns. Mary could hear their low, confused and frightened sighs, drifting through the waves. Like a herd of frightened cows, they were hair-triggered, ready at a moment, to be spooked into a stampede.

Mary didn't have any *personal* feelings, about any of this – it was all simply empirical awareness. Just as her aggressive posture wasn't attitude, so much as a dominant animal's reaction to a highly congested area of similarly agitated rivals – who, after having been run out of one feeding area, now found themselves being run out of – or perhaps *cornered*-into – another.

Yet, that extra little spark of awareness, that slight tick in her personality, had given Mary that instinctual strategy of a guerrilla.

Mary did not plan, she did not plot, but she *did* sneak. And when her aggressive instincts were activated, she was a shark that would go low, and she would hover, right where she couldn't be seen.

Hence her nickname – she always came up from behind.

All those instincts were activated at that moment.

No shark deliberately targeted human prey, and Mary did not now.

Truthfully, Mary shouldn't even have been hungry – she'd gorged on whale meat until she was sated, and then she had gorged again.

But there was hunger, and then there was instinctive response. Scientists along the coast had wondered why, in recent years, seal carcasses had washed on shore, bitten by sharks but not eaten.

Mary knew – it meant that the local white sharks had found a whale carcass somewhere, and eaten their fill.

Great Whites go *hunting* because of hunger. They *attack* when that instinctual button is activated – the shark simply saw the shadow up above.

Just as Mary did today.

She swam into the bay, already posturing – half-cocked.

Ironically, the young man sitting on the surfboard, waiting idly for his wave, had heard about the attacks. As would be reported the next day by his girlfriend, his logic had been that, since shark attacks were so rare, that meant the odds of it happening *again* were so small as to make it *extra* safe.

Ah well. Nature didn't abide a fool.

And neither did Bloody Marry.

The young man was never even consciously aware of anything except being struck by something heavy – like a car, except from below.

There was half-a-second's last-thought where he looked around for a boat.

His body was never found, but his board washed ashore, bitten in half, less than a mile down the sand from the beached whales.

The beachcomber that found it held the bite-mark up next to one of the dead cachalots, comparing the bites on the hide – a semi-circle, nearly thirty-inches across.

That picture was under headlines the next day.

CHAPTER 6

When Lauren checked her phone that morning, she saw several messages. One from her father, one from Lieutenant Hendricks, and one more from that chirpy newsgirl, Lacey Chase.

All on the same subject.

On top – flashing *urgent* – there was a message from her assistant, Nancy. When she clicked, it brought up a picture of a surfboard with a bite taken out of it – held up against another enormous bite on the carcass of a beached sperm whale.

The link told the story succinctly enough, accompanied by video.

Which meant the press was already on the scene.

Lauren shut her eyes. As a shark-advocate, it always made it harder when one of them killed somebody.

Particularly, now that she was second-guessing her own position on the subject.

A second message popped up from the Institute, instructing her to head directly to the beach.

Lauren's modest injuries were on the mend and she had been due back at work this morning – to the remarkably unsympathetic impatience of her supervisor, a woman named Cylvia Brown, who not only ran the Institute, but functioned as Lauren's department head.

Ms. Brown considered Lauren's injuries the equivalent of wrecking a car, driving drunk on company time, and let it be known, in no uncertain terms, that she viewed her presence on that ill-fated charter, unprofessional and exploitive.

Cylvia Brown was also scandalized over *Sharks and Babes*.

After Lauren had gotten her doctorate, Cylvia had remarked, "Not all of us work through college taking off their clothes."

Lauren had repeated the remark to Carson who pointed out it was coming from a woman barely five-feet tall, with no noticeably feminine traits.

Assistant Nancy referred to her generically as 'The Bitch', with the formal capitals.

But for Lauren, it was more than a personality thing. Cylvia came from an academic world of dogma and doctrine.

Lauren herself didn't believe in science as a life-philosophy. She'd trained in its discipline, but her interest in the sea was spiritual.

Cylvia, by Lauren's measure, was handicapped by knowledge without the virtue of experience, and therefore no perspective.

Lauren believed in being *part* of the natural world, not antiseptic from it. And she found she rather resented the judgmentalism of a Cylvia Brown, whose priorities seemed those of the disciplinarian – the authoritarian who would see that doctrine was honored.

Lauren did what she did because she loved it. That kind of joylessness was beyond her.

To experience the ocean was her way of experiencing *life*.

Unfortunately, just lately, it was also reminding her that the opposite was true.

Death was nature too – often brutal and cruel.

She'd gotten a text last night from Lieutenant Shaw's ex-wife – funeral date and time.

Lauren still remembered Shaw's handsome, exasperated face, as his thirty-foot port-security-boat had pulled up beside Carson's little outboard, out past the shipping lanes, all those years ago.

As she'd explained in his office, back on shore, it hadn't been *her* idea.

"But you were *there*, weren't you?" he said

It was the first time they'd met the lieutenant, but definitely not the last.

Now he was gone.

And then this morning, another surfer.

Two isolated incidents of attacks in three days, not counting the charter boat.

And Rhonda was gone.

That changed things a bit, concerning what Lauren thought she knew about the situation at Surf Shore.

Culling out one animal was not going to make the area safe. Today's incident left no doubt.

On Lauren's word, Cylvia Brown had already gone to the city, with that official statement from the Institute. The city, naturally, was not happy. Surf Shore without surfing was pretty much a death-knell for the town's economy.

But this was not a JAWS scenario – they weren't looking at a single rogue animal.

In point of fact, even Rhonda would not have qualified as a 'rogue' shark – as in, the theory that a shark develops a taste for humans and becomes a habitual man-killer like a bear or a lion. That simply didn't happen with sharks.

But sharks *did* demonstrate different personalities, and some were more pugnacious and dominant than others. Even these individuals didn't target humans specifically, but if you happened to be in their water, your odds of getting hit jumped from astronomical, to probable.

You would, of course, still be an enormously small statistic.

A bitten-in-half statistic.

Lauren was unhappy having to say so. The 'rogue shark' myth had taken a long time to discredit, and this sounded similar enough to undo all that positive change in public perception.

But she couldn't deny the danger. And the two-year patterns were very suggestive. Great Whites were very ritualized in their migration habits. It was not inconceivable that the same aggressive female could be back in the same waters repeatedly.

It was, actually, a documented fact. Suspect number one, the recently-deceased Big Rhonda, was sighted multiple times, on both film and photograph, during each of those fatal years. Lauren had filmed her personally, and had, in fact, started to become convinced she *was* the problem animal. And she may still have been.

Except, now they knew Big Rhonda was far from alone in the waters off Surf Shore.

Even if Rhonda herself *had* been responsible for all the attacks before today, including the ones on the whales, they simply couldn't overlook the fact that the concentration of sharks in the area was suddenly twice what they had previously believed.

Lauren had spent the better part of this season in the Farallons – normally shark season. Except it had been dead – dead like it had been after that famous incident all those years ago – an on-camera assault of a Great White shark.

By an orca.

Orcinus orca. The killer whale.

Orcas had been seen at the Farallons this year too. And again, the sharks were gone.

In both cases, there had been little doubt that the sharks had vacated the area, in retreat from the orcas. What was not known, was where they went.

But at least this year, it was Surf Shore – a place where researchers hadn't even realized that a full-fledged population already existed. Until Lauren herself had discovered that new seal colony, it was believed the sharks were just passing through.

Now they had been joined by the ousted refugees from the Farallons.

But the orcas had announced their presence off Surf Shore as well.

As Lauren drove along the coast, she looked out over the ocean. The waves were crashy-bangy this morning.

Rather like a bubbling cauldron.

And as she circled the bend, she saw the first of the beached whales.

Lauren let out a slow, unconscious whistle between her teeth.

There were a *lot* of them. And they were *big*. Not blues, but probably fin whales, which could top eighty-feet. It looked like a whole pod – more than a dozen.

A news helicopter circled above – the same station as the late producer/reporter David Templeton, who had charted his now-infamous three-hour tour.

Lauren wondered if Lacey Chase was on-board the chopper or perhaps waiting to ambush her at the beach.

Nancy had texted Lauren to meet her at the southern point. The stretch of beach ran approximately five miles, split in spots by rocky outcroppings, and bordered by two commercial docks. As she approached the south beach, Lauren saw an entire second pod, languished on shore – at least a dozen more whales, lined nearly all the way to the southern dock.

Lauren pulled to a stop.

Besides the second grouping of fin whales, there were three members of a sperm whale pod – two adults, probably female, and one calf.

Out on the beach, there was a congestion of reporters surrounding the three cachalots.

"These animals," Nancy's text had read, "didn't beach themselves."

Parking her car, Lauren slipped discreetly down to the sand, keeping an eye out for Lacey Chase, who was the only one who might recognize her.

She spotted Nancy, hovered beside the largest whale, as if guarding it, even as random beach folk paused to take selfies, while reporters rolled cameras, snapping still-shots. She waved as she saw Lauren.

They would have to get the area cordoned off. Lauren sent a text to Cylvia Brown, asking her to call the city.

But now she could see the reason for the extra attention, and why Nancy had called her down here. Unlike the beached baleens, these whales were covered with shark bites.

BIG shark bites.

That, of course, didn't mean the sharks had killed them, but it did mean these animals had died at sea, and had been floating for at least a couple of days.

Ordinarily, it wouldn't even have occurred to Lauren that a shark might be involved in their deaths.

But Nancy was right, these animals didn't die beaching themselves.

Lauren kicked off her shoes, shuffling past the mulling reporters, like a random gawker, as she trundled down into the surf where the big whale rocked slowly, as if snoring, with the incoming tide.

"Lauren!" Nancy called. "Look here!" She was waving urgently. Lauren sighed. Nancy was a good kid, but she was a bit of a puppy – an irritating kid-sister that just wanted to *follow* you everywhere. Lauren prepared herself to be patient.

Nancy's face was flush and excited, pointing to the big sperm whale's cannibalized flipper.

"Look," she said, pushing up on the heavy fin to show where the muscle and tendon had been severed – likely a crippling injury. "This animal has been attacked."

Lauren studied the wound. It was hard to define the original cut, because so much of the surrounding tissue had been eaten away in two-foot, cup-shaped bites.

But it *did* look like a deliberately targeted strike.

Megalodon was the last true whale-killer shark, the largest in a line of 'mega-tooth' species. Analogous to saber-toothed cats versus modern lions, they were an extinct sister group to the modern makos that evolved into today's *Carcharodon carcharias* – the Great White shark.

Within the scaled-down modern ecology, the general scientific consensus was that there just weren't enough calories in the food-chain to support a predatory shark that ate whales.

Or was there?

Lauren had already been speculating whether Rhonda's behavior towards whales, and by extension, towards boats, was the case of an isolated, aggressive individual, or if it might represent a behavioral shift – maybe one related to size.

Perhaps, it was an ingrained instinct that was there all along.

There were some big sharks out there. With the population evacuated from the Farallons also crammed in, competition for fast little seals grew fierce – and in the presence of whales... well, why not?

There was something potentially even *more* telling in the case of the targeted orca.

Was *that* an isolated case? Or was it the natural reaction of an individual having attained sufficient size?

Or, was it the population itself, reaching a sufficiently robust level? No different than an ant colony that grows big enough to take on the termite mound two trees over.

If they were correct in their estimates that the population of sharks was at least a third, possibly double, what they had believed, because of an also-unquantified population of pinnipeds, it suggested that *all* populations were being comfortably supported.

Perhaps it wasn't that the ocean didn't have whales to eat, but that orcas were eating them first, and *that* was why there was no Megalodon anymore.

But animals of indeterminate growth got big when you fed them. These sharks were well-fed.

And when you got right down to it, an animal took big prey once it got big enough itself.

That was at least one of the things wrong in the waters off Surf Shore.

As a life-long conservationist, with a particular emphasis on Great Whites, Lauren wondered what responsibility *she* had to bear.

She knew what Cody thought.

To her credit, Lauren had promptly forwarded her concerns to the Institute. Even Cylvia Brown, replying via e-mail and scornful at first, couldn't help but recognize that this wasn't just about attacks on humans – which were tragic, but not ecologically new or inexplicable. But they had a Great White that had attacked *and* killed at least two whales, including an orca.

And beyond that, two boats.

But now was it possible, Lauren wondered, that a white shark could have actually taken out a sperm whale?

The flipper injury was typical of a smaller animal attacking a larger one, like a wolf crippling an elk.

Or even more than one? For a moment, her imagination ran wild, picturing a piranha-like assault on a whale by a hundred sharks.

She shook her head, jettisoning the image quickly as ridiculous. Sharks simply weren't capable of coordinated attacks. Shark bites on dead whales were hardly unusual – almost every carcass that floated down the coast had them, and Lauren could clearly see most of the bites on these whales were postmortem.

Except for that flipper bite.

There were a couple of tell-tale signs she was specifically looking for. Because, while white sharks didn't attack large prey in coordination, she was very aware of another ocean predator who did.

And as Nancy led her to where the massive cachalot's jaws splayed out on the sand, she found just the sign she was looking for.

"Look at this," Nancy said, indicating where the toothed lower jaw had been torn away on one side.

Inside the open gullet, the tongue had been almost surgically removed, as opposed to the cup-shaped chomps of the white shark bites – similar to what Lauren had been able to ascertain from the flipper wound.

She exchanged glances with Nancy, who nodded.

They both jumped as a voice behind them spoke aloud.

"I take it you recognize that."

They both turned to find a man standing behind them. He nodded to the dead whale.

"Orcas," he said.

The man smiled, and his eyes wrinkled into crows-feet, revealing him as older than he looked at first glance.

As he stepped forward to greet them, extending his hand, Lauren saw he was leaning on a cane, although, he did so as an athlete recovering from an injury, using it to hop and vault himself along on his good leg.

Lauren found herself reflexively attracted to him, in the way she occasionally was to older men. She guessed him in his mid-forties, but with the trim form of an abalone diver.

"You're Doctor Lauren Palmer," he said. "I called your office. They said you were here. I'm Doctor Peter Nichols."

Lauren had started to reach for his offered hand, but at the mention of his name, she stopped.

CHAPTER 7

Lauren had gotten the message that a *Doctor* Peter Nichols had called.

It was an unpopular name among the California activist community, particularity in regards to captive orcas and the sea-parks. From what Lauren knew, he was considered an expert-for-hire.

Why on Earth would *he* be calling her?

Although, as she looked at the surgically torn jaw, so different from the piranha-like shark bites, she could assume her answer.

Peter Nichols' brows raised slightly at her half-raised arm, before he simply reached the last few inches, taking her hand for a brief shake, before letting her go.

"Call me Pete," he said.

In the manner of one who was used to it, he skipped quickly past any awkwardness by simply ignoring it. Balancing his one good leg in the wet sand, he bent to inspect the cachalot's torn jaw.

"Ahhh, Corky," he sighed.

Lauren and Nancy exchanged glances.

"Who's 'Corky'?" Nancy asked.

Pete smiled wistfully. "Corky is a friend of mine. She's a female killer whale. And I'm pretty sure this is her handiwork."

"She is also," he said, "the reason that I'm here."

He glanced over his shoulder, where a couple of the reporters were eyeing them curiously, and Lauren frowned as she now saw Lacey Chase among them.

The chirpy little reporterette waved urgently, and not a second later, Lauren heard her phone beep.

"Oh Lord." She tapped Nancy on her shoulder. "*You*. Keep those reporters away from me."

Nancy eyed the crowd nervously. "They're going to want some kind of statement."

Lauren nodded. "So give them one."

Nancy looked doubtfully between Pete and the dead whale.

"Um. What should I tell them?"

"Tell them what we know," Lauren said, with a touch of impatience.

Hearing the tone, Nancy ducked discreetly away.

Lauren turned to Pete.

"So," she said, "*Doctor* Nichols. I was surprised to hear from you. You have a reputation."

"As an expert-for-hire?" Pete nodded agreeably. "Well, that still makes me an expert, doesn't it? One worth hiring."

"So who hired you this time?" Lauren asked.

"Actually," Pete said dryly, "this is really more about who hired me *last* time. I assume you know who *that* was?"

Lauren did. It had been a big scandal, two states up in Washington, several months ago.

In fact, the last Lauren had heard, it was *still* a pretty big scandal – the legal ramifications had yet to be fully determined.

Pete's former employer had been the late philanthropist-billionaire, Ted Ryder, who had set up his own killer whale rehab facility – a private operation that had been widely criticized by activists as a rich-man's aquarium.

Of course, the operation had ended in disaster, and the captive whales had escaped into the open ocean.

For the activist movement, that might actually have been considered a happy ending.

Unfortunately, several people died in the incident.

And one of them happened to be the governor of the state, on-site of a facility owned by his biggest donor.

By all indications, it was the orcas who had caused the death of Governor Kirkland and his staff – among others – by sinking their boat in the stormy water, as they had ferried across the bay.

Pete Nichols had been caretaker of this facility. With his reputation already in question, there had been an initial mob on social media ready to lynch him for it.

However, as details of the story unfolded, it turned out the security of the operation had been compromised by Ted Ryder himself.

One night, he had simply gone out and unlocked the gates.

Pete himself was later asked on camera to speculate *why*.

"I think he just wanted to see them free," he had replied.

Lauren had seen that clip on the news, and found the remark hauntingly poignant.

In any event, Ryder would never be held accountable. He had since taken his own life.

As caretaker, Pete's own responsibility, and possible negligence, were still being determined by the state.

Between that and what she had heard about his anti-conservationist leanings, Lauren reminded herself that, good-looking with a charming smile or not, he was a possible felon.

She eyed him directly.

"Your 'friends' are implicated in human deaths," Lauren said.

"Actually," Pete corrected, "*one* orca was implicated. Bruno. A big male transient who was shot and killed at the facility."

Lauren nodded.

"So why are you still out on the ocean following them?"

Pete tapped his cane on the carcass of the dead whale.

"Because, Doctor Palmer," he said, "these are not the first orca-kills I've seen this season."

He shook his head regretfully.

"I've actually been following a trail of slaughtered whales down the coast for the last several months."

Lauren frowned. She knew the big transient orcas occasionally took whales. But going after the larger species, even baleens, was something of a rare event.

"How many?" she asked.

"Two dozen," Pete said. "Maybe more."

"Two dozen...?"

Lauren blinked. She had been expecting to hear five or six. Two dozen meant the slaughter of entire pods. Endangered species all of them.

Why? Why would orcas *do* that?

"And that," Pete said, "doesn't count beachings."

He nodded past the dead, shark-bitten cachalots to the stranded pod of fin-whales that littered the rest of the beach.

"You think your captive escapees are responsible?" Lauren said. "Why would you think this is their work more than any wild pod?"

Pete glanced back to where Nancy was dutifully keeping the reporters' attention. Lauren heard Lacey Chase's voice rising impatiently above the others.

For a moment, Nancy stood up, shoulders squared, and Lauren was surprised to see the cover-girl reporter actually back off.

Pete grinned. "I like your assistant."

Lauren would not be charmed.

'Pete let it go.

"How much do you know about killer whale eco-types?" he asked.

Lauren wasn't an academic-level specialist, but she had interest.

"I know they speak different languages."

"And hunt different prey," Pete said. "Because of the lifestyles associated with that, they have evolved into entirely different cultures. But these escapees are animals who have been living together in captivity for a long time, and now they're traveling together."

Lauren nodded slowly, beginning to understand.

"They're hunting a wide variety of prey."

Pete nodded approvingly.

"Very good, Doctor." He tapped the whale carcass with his cane again. "There are two transients in the group, and three pack-ice orcas. All known whale hunters. But Corky is the lead female, and she's from a resident pod. And you combine the playfulness and activity-level of a resident with a whale hunter's targets..."

He shrugged, nodding to the three slaughtered whales.

"They're killing for the fun of it," Lauren said.

Pete nodded.

"Most advanced predators do. Lions and wolves learn hunting and killing as play. It's a fiction that only humans kill for pleasure.

"But," he continued, "there's a symbiosis at work. Orca cultures develop around the food they hunt, and so there are reasons they behave like they do. Wild transient pods don't go after big sperm whales for the thrill of it, and they don't over-hunt. A fish-eating resident isn't getting all the calories that come with warm-blooded prey, so they tend to *always* be on the hunt. Simple things like that make a difference."

He tapped the whale carcasses with his cane.

"A big difference," he said.

Okay, Lauren thought, he had her attention. Whatever his reputation, she found herself responding and being led by his banter.

Which made sense – he was an animal handler. She reminded herself of that, lest she find herself being handled.

"So what can *I* do for you, Doctor Nichols?"

Pete's eyes again cut briefly towards the press.

"Well," he said, keeping his voice low, "I understand you've had an unusual orca incident yourself, recently."

Lauren's eyes narrowed. That was one element of the charter wreck that hadn't been reported – the part where Big Rhonda had been taken by an orca pod.

How did *Pete* know?

"A killer whale hit a white shark," Lauren said. "But it was a wild pod. I saw it." She shook her head. "And it wasn't predation. The shark had taken one of their calves."

Pete's brows raised.

"A white shark took an *orca* calf?"

Lauren nodded.

"It was a *big* shark. A big *aggressive* shark."

"Did anyone else see this?"

Lauren paused. She had started to say a whole boat-full. Then she realized there was only one person besides herself who was still alive.

She debated saying his name. Of all people, he was one who might not appreciate it. And their history was frosty at best.

"Cody Martin," she said, finally. "He saw the calf. He also saw the orcas take out the shark."

"Is he someone I can speak to?"

Lauren shrugged doubtfully.

"He's a little intense."

"Well," a woman's voice said from behind them, "you should be used to that, shouldn't you, Pete?"

Pete paused, his eyes blinking briefly shut, before he turned to where a car had parked, right at the edge of the sand.

A woman was standing by her open door, posed and smiling. And where Pete's grin had been good-natured, with the wrinkling of crows-feet, this woman's smile was sharp, immaculately manicured, and deliberate.

Lauren actually found herself impressed, even a bit intimidated – the woman cut the image of the ruthlessly smart, supermodel-CEO – the sort of boss known to crack the whip.

Pete breathed through his teeth, "Ahhhh, *damn*."

The woman was still smiling as she approached, but she didn't extend her hand.

"Hello, Kate," Pete said.

CHAPTER 8

"Kate Foster," Pete introduced, "meet Doctor Lauren Palmer."

Now Kate extended her hand, and Lauren shook it, remembering how Carson described her – not critically – as a woman who got a *lot* done with her ass.

Carson, who said this while prepping for a free swim with a tiger shark, had slapped her own taut, barely-clad tush.

"Whatever works, honey."

Kate Foster was well-known as a fundraiser, someone who dated donors and politicians.

And in point of fact, Lauren recalled that Kate had been dating Washington's late Governor Stuart Kirkland.

Before he had died, there had even been buzz among the activists who most directly benefited from Kate's activities – mostly orca and cetacean-related groups – that she was zeroing in on Ted Ryder's money as a source of direct funding.

When it came to money, the professional idealists were as cynical as anyone, and the general consensus was that Governor Kirkland was getting old. As much leverage as that relationship had given Kate in regards to her various causes, it was becoming a finite window, once Kirkland termed-out.

Kate, to coin Carson's phrase – again, not disparagingly – would soon be looking to trade-up.

That was before the escape at the facility.

In terms of legality, Kate's own involvement had been presented in the news as periphery. Besides, the press *liked* her. Even though she originally came into the picture as the hot-young-stuff, they treated her like the Governor's wife.

Although, Lauren *had* heard Kate's name in the news again, just recently. It seemed the new attorney general, appointed after Governor Kirkland's death – a severe and humorless woman, commonly known by her full-name, *Agnes Walker*, and who rather resembled a Puritan gerbil – was campaigning on a no-nonsense, anti-corruption platform, and looked at the high-profile Ted Ryder case as a vehicle.

It was further presumed, among the activist community, that if this proved to be true, Kate Foster would give her a fight.

On short acquaintance, Lauren was inclined to agree.

"It's good to meet you, Doctor Palmer," Kate said. "It's actually *you* I came down here to meet." She smiled politely, before turning her attention to Pete.

"Doctor Nichols," she said, "is a complete surprise."

"A happy surprise, I'm sure," Pete said.

Kate smiled, just as if it were so.

"You're looking good, Pete. No more casts."

Pete held up his cane. "I can swim better than I can walk, but I'm working on it."

Kate seemed to hesitate – an unaccustomed moment, Lauren was sure.

"Listen," she said, "I'm sorry I haven't called. Or never came by while you were hurt. My lawyers tell me I'm not supposed to talk to you."

"I'm sure my lawyers would say the same thing, if I had them," Pete agreed. "So, what *are* you doing here, Kate?"

She nodded apologetically. "Well, as I said. I'd actually like to talk to Doctor Palmer. *Privately.*"

Pete smiled. "Don't worry. I'm leaving."

He turned to Lauren and handed her his card. "Please call me," he said. "I'd like to compare notes."

Lauren looked at him, so deceptively reasonable. But that was the point of an expert-for-hire.

"I'll call you," she agreed.

Pete nodded to Kate.

"Be good," he told her.

"You too, Pete."

He turned to leave.

Kate paused, looking out over the beached carcasses. After a moment, she called after him.

"It's them, isn't it?"

Pete stopped, leaning on his cane, looking back over his shoulder.

"I don't know *that*, for sure," he said. "But it's definitely orcas."

He tipped an imaginary hat as he turned and trundled off, shuffling over the hump of dry sand to the street. He seemed to be laboring more on his cane now, and Lauren wondered if it was for Kate's benefit.

Now that he was out of earshot, Kate smiled confidentially.

"I'm sorry. First impressions. I take it you've only just met Doctor Nichols? What do you think?"

"I'm still making up my mind. I guess you two have history?"

"Good and bad," Kate allowed. "Like with any man. He's honest about what he believes. I'll vouch for that."

"What can I do for you, Ms. Foster?"

Kate smiled. "Well," she said. "To the point. I would like to use your story as a promotional vehicle."

"*My* story?"

Kate leaned close, "I got a little tip from an activist friend, who also happens to be a municipal court judge. She told me all the details that haven't been made public."

Lauren blinked. Municipal court?

Oh no.

There was only one thing *that* could mean.

"Mr. Cody Martin," Kate said. "From what I'm told, he's your hero. Why haven't you told anyone?"

Lauren had actually been completely unprepared for this particular conversation. There had been enough distractions that she'd half-forgotten this part of the story was only waiting to break.

It wasn't until that moment that she realized she might actually *be* the story – as in eyes-of-the-world upon her.

Her. Her little life, suddenly all over the globe.

Not like *Sharks and Babes.* That was an on-line following in scuba masks – it wasn't like she was going to be recognized on the street. Not by her *face*, anyway.

For a moment, Lauren actually felt the impulse to run, to just beg Kate off and not talk any further.

But she supposed it was coming anyway.

"Honestly, Ms. Foster..."

"*Kate.*"

Lauren smiled patiently. "*Kate.* Cody and I have our own history. And I think I can safely say he wouldn't appreciate me talking about him."

Kate was nodding.

"I see," she said, taking out her phone. "I did a little research on Mr. Martin. Apparently, he got in a little trouble over your friend, Carson?"

Kate pulled up a mug-shot. Next to it, was a picture of another young man, with two black eyes, and a distorted and darkly-swollen nose.

"Carson's ex-boyfriend," Lauren said. "Pre-med. I can't remember his name. Carson told me it was a counter-punch."

"But Carson's dad knows the mayor. *And* the news-editor of the local rag, and its TV affiliate. And her dad never liked Cody, did he?"

Lauren frowned. "What's your point? Kate?"

Kate's lips seemed to perk at Lauren's brief terseness, setting her hook.

"I'm saying maybe you owe the guy to tell a better story about him."

"What exactly do you have in mind?"

"Well," Kate said, "I actually had three projects in mind. The first would be a documentary, one in which I would like to use you, and your

Institute, to film on these waters. Secondly, I would like to use this documentary as a springboard for a dramatization. I've already got a major studio willing to donate a crew and equipment."

A major studio. Lauren absorbed this tidbit quietly. What kind of clout did it take to get *those* phone calls made?

She was also rather numb at the prospect of someone actually *playing* her in a movie.

"And the third thing?" Lauren asked.

"Well," Kate said, nodding to the carcasses strewn up the beach, "I'd like to do something about these whales."

Lauren braced herself. There had been some pretty stupid things done with beached whales in the past. Up in Oregon, a beached sperm whale was once dynamited by some dimwit local official. The blast had sent chunks the size of car engines flying for blocks.

"Beached whales are always a problem," Kate said, "because they're basically several tons of meat, spoiling in the hot sun. It's man-power and resources to get rid of them. And you've got thirty animals beached over a few short miles. I want to tow them offshore."

Lauren nodded. Okay, so far.

Kate eyed her expectantly. "And what happens to whale carcasses at sea?"

Lauren turned and looked at the cup-shaped bites on the beached whales.

"They get eaten by sharks," she said.

"It's also my understanding that you have more than your share of sharks in these waters."

Lauren considered. "I think that's fair enough to say."

"So, we perform a public service, by cleaning the carcasses off the beaches. We perform an ecological service by not letting these dead animals go to waste. And maybe we even draw some of these sharks off your beaches."

Now Lauren frowned. Thirty whales? All in the same, already over-stimulated area?

In these waters, it was a virtual beacon for a food-orgy.

Of course, any doubts she might have entertained were quickly dwarfed, as Kate put the cherry on top.

"The studio," she said, "is particularly interested in filming this part. Especially once I told them that many of these sharks are approaching twenty-feet long."

Kate grinned broadly.

"I plan on broadcasting it live-stream. I even expect to sell tickets. I'm thinking of calling it 'Feeding Frenzy'. Or maybe, 'Great White Feeding Frenzy'? What do you think?"

"Well," Lauren said slowly, "I think it sounds incredibly invasive. And exploitive. Not to mention dangerous."

She shook her head. "Seriously, Ms. Fost... *Kate*. The last time I was out there, a single shark hit our charter boat and sunk it. That's something I've never seen or heard of before. You're talking about deliberately stirring up a very hazardous situation."

"We're getting a bigger boat, Doctor Palmer," Kate said, her smile narrowing slightly.

Lauren felt the force of the woman's personality. She also felt herself being studied – she had been approached as a mark, but the moment she was perceived as an obstacle, she'd better watch for rototiller blades.

"Listen, honey," Kate said, "I've seen your little videos. Those were shoe-string."

Now Kate took her by the shoulder – a gesture of sisterhood. And Lauren was certain she'd talked to a lot of scientists and researchers in just this manner – most often those of an activist/conservationist bent. Just like Lauren herself.

"What's a scientist starved for, more than anything?" Kate asked, and then answered. "Resources. Money. Always. Do you understand the opportunity I'm offering you and your Institute?"

Lauren didn't answer, but she did find herself wondering what the dour Cylvia Brown would say.

"I'm sorry, Ms.... Kate." Lauren shook her head. "I'm not wild about this incident – my *life* – being exploited. Not for a documentary, and certainly not for a straight-to-cable docudrama. As far as this little stunt you're planning, I think it's an extremely bad idea. And if going forward, you need my sign-off, I'm afraid I can't, in good conscience, give it to you."

Kate nodded amicably enough.

"Actually," she said, "I don't really need your sign-off. I was hoping to bring you on-board, but the truth is, I already bought the rights to the story."

"Bought them? From whom?"

"I got them from Cody Martin. He signed the contract yesterday."

"He *what*?"

"For both the movie and the documentary," Kate said. "Of course, yesterday, these whales hadn't even beached yet. I'll have to call him and tell him his slice just got bigger. I'm sure he'll be happy to hear that."

Now she rooted around in her purse.

"Here," she said, handing Lauren her card. "I hope we can work together. Or at least not be at cross-purposes. Give me a call if you change your mind."

Kate turned to go, but paused on her heel, turning back.

"You know, I wasn't kidding about your friend Cody." She held up her phone with his mugshot still on the screen. "At the very least, *he* might think it'd be worth something to have you set the record straight."

"Cody and I have said all we needed to," Lauren replied. "Thank you, Ms. Foster."

Kate nodded at the deliberate surname, and turned to go. Lauren glanced over to where Nancy was now simply lecturing the lingering reporters like a tour-guide, showing the shapes of the shark-bites on the whale carcasses, posing for pictures. Lacey Chase was actually popping gum.

Lauren looked down at Kate's card in her hand, and sighed.

Cody had signed off on the whole thing, going public with what just happened to be *her* story too – and all the angst about public exposure had just suddenly been yanked out of her control. *And* he took money for it.

Lauren wondered if he'd done it just to piss her off.

All things considered, that wasn't an unreasonable speculation.

Kate mentioned a municipal judge had been her contact. There was only one way Lauren could think of where that would have led a trail to Cody.

Lauren had been a bit cooked that Cody hadn't come to see her in the hospital. It wasn't for almost two days that she had found out why.

The reason was, he'd been in jail.

After they'd arrived back at the dock, on the day of the charter boat accident, they had been met by emergency vehicles and police. The Coast Guard, including Lieutenant Shaw, were still back at the wreck-site. The ambulance and cops had arrived without knowing all the details, and Lauren was quickly carted off to the emergency room.

But as she was being loaded into the ambulance, she had caught the tail-end of Cody and the police – Cody's voice rising, "For God's sake, I'm supposed to be making a statement to the goddamn Coast Guard!"

Then the paramedics had shut the door and she hadn't heard any more.

As it turned out, the dock foreman had pointed Cody out. In his hurry to get out to the wreck-site – where Lauren's oxygen tank was ticking away, seventy-feet down – Cody had bowled past the crotchety docks-man, knocking him to the ground. The foreman had called the police.

And, of course, Cody's arrest record, for punching out a pre-med a year ago, popped right up – a prior assault. And the police, who didn't know or care about any nautical incident, had taken him off to jail.

It was the second time Cody had made the news. Once Lauren had finally heard about it from Lieutenant Hendricks, she'd searched the story and brought up a security-camera video of Cody knocking down the foreman as he ran past.

Of course, Lieutenant Quinton Shaw wasn't around to vouch for him. And none of the other guardsmen even thought to mention Cody after Shaw himself got hit.

Cody just sort of got forgotten.

By the time Lauren discovered the story, he had already been released. There had been a news-blip yesterday, with a rare statement from the judge on the case, announcing the dismissal – presumably the same judge who had called Kate Foster.

Cody, by Lauren's math, would have been in jail from the time that they carted her off, until just after noon yesterday – almost three days.

And she had been the one who was mad at *him* for not visiting her.

Oh, there was going to be *no* talking to him.

CHAPTER 9

Pete had to admit, Kate Foster was a force to reckon with.

"Anything ever happen with her?"

Pete glanced over at his friend – well, *colleague* – Tommy Larson, known as the 'whale-whisperer'. Or more precisely, the *orca*-whisperer.

"There might have, if I hadn't been hurt," Pete said, "Not that it would have mattered. Push comes to shove, she is who she is. She needs a new sponsor. It wasn't like *that* was ever going to be me."

Tommy chuckled. "I didn't say mate for life."

Pete ignored him. "Besides," he said, "I think she wanted to be down here, near the community. A support group, lest anything untoward come out of the investigations back in Washington."

"What about you?" Tommy asked. "Are you still in the glue?"

Pete shrugged. "If they want me to be."

Truth be told, for Pete, his own personal judgment was never more than a second's doubt away. As far as the state? Ultimately, it would be up to others to decide what his penance should be.

As on-site orca-caretaker, some degree of responsibility absolutely lay upon his own shoulders. He had underestimated the animals in his care.

Although, in his own defense, with orcas, that was easy to do.

Kate Foster was easy to underestimate as well. He had seen trouble coming with that one, and he had *vastly* underestimated her.

In this one instance, however, there was something Kate was unaware that he knew.

Pete was privy to a little orca jail-break plot of Kate's own.

The governor's daughter had been killed in that debacle at the facility as well. Her boat had been sunk outside the compound on the open ocean.

Maggie Kirkland had been with a group of orca-activists who had apparently been planning to blow the bay-gate.

Unfortunately, the orcas had beaten them to it. And Bruno had found them.

Pete was pretty sure it was Bruno.

In the wake of the governor's death, none of the logistics had been overly analyzed. But Pete happened to have discovered that Kate Foster's visit to Ted Ryder's facility that night was intended as cover for Maggie Kirkland's operation.

Pete had kept this little tidbit private – even from Kate herself.

Like it or not, they'd bonded over their ordeal – she'd whacked an eight-meter orca with a boat-hook as it chomped his leg. He supposed he was willing to *not* call the cops on her when he found the text message to Maggie Kirkland on her phone.

Pete was, however, wondering if someone at the state had followed the trail of Maggie Kirkland's own texting. At the time, the cause of the incident was considered obvious, and any further investigation buried as needlessly embarrassing to the families.

The new AG, however, seemed to be digging. It would seem logical that Maggie Sawyer's electronic dots would have to connect to Kate's own.

The only living conspirator.

There had been a couple of calls from the state informing Pete that the AG's office would be in contact, and that his testimony might be subpoenaed.

He supposed he could play dumb.

In his current state of mind, that somehow seemed the right thing.

On the other hand, he hadn't been threatened with prison time yet.

It was rather terrifying when your future suddenly lay in the hands of another person's discretion, be it whim or judgment, with no reason to put your best interests at heart.

He tried to imagine Kate in the same position.

Pete considered himself very fortunate it was provable Ryder himself had rigged the gates to the orca pens. Kate may have pulled him out of an orca's jaws, but she would definitely throw him under the bus. *That* lady wasn't doing jail-time.

So, perhaps it was best it all ended like it did.

Except it *hadn't* ended, and here they were again. He hoped he didn't find himself between Kate and a bus.

Pete hopped experimentally on his still-healing leg – a parting gift from Bruno.

"All told," he said, "I think I came off lucky."

"Yeah," Tommy said. "I had a one-eyed dog named Lucky."

You wouldn't guess it by looking at him, but Tommy Larson was, by Pete's estimation, the foremost authority on killer whales in the world.

Orca trainers who had met him said Tommy could interact with problem-orcas they had taken years to train.

Pete, who himself had served time at the sea-parks, agreed.

The sea-parks were a time of his life he had very mixed feelings about – a pursuit he had come to out of love, but followed by disillusionment, even as his own basic wonder grew.

Perhaps worse was the cynicism that inevitably corroded the edges as his unpopular voice was villainized by those he once trusted and believed.

Truth to tell, he'd never really gotten along that well with humans, anyway.

The sea-parks had given him interaction and understanding of orcas, so it was hard to condemn his time there entirely.

In fact, Tommy Larson was probably the only person he would cede to on the subject – not because he had any scientific reason to trust his methods, but because the damn fool seemed to interact with wild pods in ways Pete had never seen.

Tommy was ten years Pete's junior, and as far as Pete was concerned, he was the most undisciplined, irresponsible, reckless, non-scientific pseudo-scientist on the planet, and had said so both publicly and to him personally.

"Yeah," Tommy had responded, "I talk to orcas all the time. They say you're full of shit."

This had been at a bar, after a day spent off the Washington coast, floating Tommy's small boat along the north Pacific migratory routes of the big transient orcas.

It was the same day Pete had come to the final and frustrating conclusion that, for whatever voodoo was at play, there were just some people who could do amazing things with animals.

Tommy was semi-famous in the northwest. Local papers had been running photographs since he was twelve – always out by himself, most often on a kayak – and always surrounded by a dozen or more six-foot black fins.

He always carried with him a flute, with which he alternately played written music, but more often just seemed to imitate the sounds of the animals around him.

These days, he claimed to be able to speak 'orca'.

Pete had made the counter-claim that it was total bullshit. He had seen footage, and yes, the orcas seemed to respond to Tommy's flute, even nosing up against him, like an orca in a sea-park. But that was really no different than a dog that learned tricks, interacting with humans – and orcas were a *much* more intelligent animal.

Wild orcas were long-known for stopping to play with people on boats, even throwing ice-chunks with their tails in imitation of a human throwing snowballs – and to the chagrin of commercial fishermen, sometimes raiding their nets and stealing fish off of their lines.

Tommy had been interacting for years with every pod that lived or passed through the limits of his travels. Pete had been of the opinion that he had basically created a big song-and-dance act, developed over time with the naturally playful and willing orcas.

Still, when you were out on the boat with him, it was a hell of a trick.

When he started on the flute, Pete had to admit, he did mimic orca-chatter very well.

But the thing that caught his ear, hearing it in person, was the way he seemed to send his voice through it – not even like a flute, so much as someone who played a pretty good harmonica.

When Tommy had tried to explain, he'd described the way notes, if played well, can lead the listener's own moods up and down, downbeat or up-tempo. They send both message and emotion.

"It's more like you don't *have* to talk," Tommy said.

Pete had been skeptical. That wasn't all that different than a dog's whine.

Although, in both cases, he supposed it *was* communication.

It was also where orcas were unique – *all* dogs whined, but the sounds of one orca eco-type, were not the same as another.

Pete had long been fascinated by the obvious differences in non-instinctive behavior among orcas. Killer whales, along with human beings, were the only species where different groups were known to possess different customs and traditions, that were taught and passed down generationally among populations.

Tommy, of course, knew the differences in the pods because he had *met* them.

He sometimes brought stereo-equipment, playing CDs, broadcast out into the ocean. All paid for by his university grant, just like the boat they'd been touring down the coast.

But on that particular day, there had been no fancy stereo, no *Who* or *Styx* – orca-favorites, according to Tommy – he had just played his flute. He didn't even use any acoustical equipment fed into the water, just played into the open air.

And damned if, within twenty minutes, a pod of orcas didn't pop their fins less than half-a-mile distant.

Tommy had laughed, and puffed out a quick riff of notes.

Pete raised a brow.

"My Bonnie lies over the Ocean?"

A moment later, a large female orca had popped up, spy-hopping not five feet away.

Tommy had reached over and patted the huge harlequin head.

"Bonnie Parker," he introduced. "After Bonnie and Clyde. 'Cuz she's a bit of a gangster. She's the lead female of the biggest transient gang on the coast."

Pete nodded, respectfully, patting the big orca above her white patch. Bonnie shifted in the water, and Pete eyed her carefully – transients were mammal eaters – seals, and sometimes whales.

Bruno, who had broken Pete's leg, had been a transient.

But on that day, at least, Bonnie seemed amiable enough.

They had followed the transient pod along the coast for the next several hours, with each member, from senior bull down to calf, stopping in to say hello, each rearing up to spy-hop, several of them breaching.

That was the thing about orcas. You could travel next to them, watch them take down giant whales, brutally assault dolphins and seals, and yet Pete felt not the slightest threat.

The incident at the facility had not changed that – those had been *captive* orcas, and almost all the known attacks on humans by killer whales were from captive individuals.

Captivity could make an orca mean.

One problem was that they were open-ocean animals in a cramped space.

The second was, they were too intelligent for a cage.

Pete could testify to it himself. Trapped in a tank, their active minds languishing, their bodies growing flabby and their fins drooping, many orcas started to suffer mental deterioration. An orca had a year, maybe two, before they started exhibiting neurotic behavior. Some dangerously so.

For a long time, the sea-parks had kept mum about the more serious incidents, with orcas nearly drowning trainers.

When Pete had first started, he had been told by the then-lead trainer, a woman who had worked with captive orcas for years, "They'll take you down to the bottom, and hold you there until the last second, because they know exactly how long before you run out of air."

Pete never had an incident like that, the special circumstance of Bruno the lone exception – possibly, he had a bit of Tommy Larson in him.

But he did believe that the effect of captivity on an orca's mind was similar to a human being in prison.

Orcas weren't unique in that regard. Many higher animals, including gorillas and chimpanzees, were known to display psychosis after isolation.

The difference was, an orca could be thirty-feet long and nine-tons. It didn't have to work very hard to let you know it wasn't happy.

There had been a number of deaths in sea-parks worldwide, mostly trainers. But all things considered, Pete was amazed it wasn't more. Captive bears and big cats often killed their trainers, but around humans, orcas seemed remarkably restrained. Even the fatal incidents amounted to moments of pique.

At least until the death of Dawn Brancheau, a trainer who had worked for years with a large transient male named Tilikum, who for some reason, one day decided to drown and dismember her.

Tilikum had been responsible for two other human deaths – another trainer, as well as an apparently drug-addled individual who had broken into the park at night and tried to go swimming – naked – with the large bull orca.

In all three cases, the victims had been mercilessly pummeled and drowned.

Bruno had similarly killed his trainer, in the tiny tank where he had been kept in Mexico. Rather than see him put down, Ted Ryder had brought him to the facility.

The big orca had responded well, even eagerly, to Pete's more humane treatment, as well as the open range of the bay.

But it had been Bruno who had led the others to escape. Bruno was also most likely responsible for all the human deaths involved.

Unfortunately, Pete couldn't prove it.

Besides his own liability, there were those that considered the accountability of the orcas themselves, and whether they were a continued threat to humans now that they were loose.

Pete had, in fact, used that very argument as a reason for not releasing them prematurely to begin with.

But Bruno had been put down. And Pete was certain none of the others posed any danger to people.

Pretty certain.

But the ecology at large...?

That was a harder case to make.

Especially, Pete thought, when the tide washed in a dramatic evidence like it had today.

It was already being reported as the largest mass beaching on the California coast this century.

Pete mourned the loss of magnificent life.

But he also worried what it might mean for his friends.

That night at the facility was the last time he'd seen them. But he had been sent pictures. The escapees were following the transient migratory route. They were recognizable by their fins.

It had been Tommy Larson who tipped him first, with a distance shot of an old male, with a drooping fin – an Antarctic eco-type, way out of his element.

Tommy had also sent him some disturbing footage of wild orcas, taken along the same route.

A fight – between members of transient and offshore pods.

Pete had never met the off-shore pods, but Tommy had – the largest was led by a senior female he called 'Calypso.' She and Bonnie had traveled the same waters for decades.

Transients were larger, but off-shore orcas traveled in greater numbers. The squabble had been scouting members, rather than a full-on clan war, but it had been brutal, with blood and injuries on both sides.

Dramatic footage, interesting to the layman – 'animals-fighting' click-bait.

Except, Pete knew that was something that simply didn't happen with orcas.

Orca pods were known for an odd sort of détente between eco-types. So-called 'killer' whales didn't fight among each other – not in the wild. It only happened in the forced proximity of captivity, where residents were known to attack transients... although, oddly, not the other way around.

Killer whale social strictures went back tens of thousands of years, each pod adapted to a specific niche of prey. Nor did different eco-types mate with each other, as again, was the case in forced proximity.

Strict adherence to these customs, over generations, allowed for an elegant harmony among different co-existing populations of the most dangerous predator in the ocean. They didn't compete over prey, or mates, or territory – the three things that ALL other animals go to war over – including humans. It was a socio-biologic evolution unique on the planet.

But now it seemed long-stranding customs were being broken, and with them, treaties that dated back before humans existed in their modern form.

Tommy had also sent the first footage of dead whales – both orca-taken, and beached, as the trail led south down the coast.

Since then, he and Pete had lived out of the boat like a tent, following the migratory path.

They'd seen no sign of Corky's pod, but found evidence of their work – dead whales, sometimes fresh.

On those occasions, Pete wondered whether Corky might be hanging about, somewhere down below.

She was the type that would – always the first to roll you over with an exuberant wave when you greeted her in the morning, her clever mind always playing diabolical pranks. Her brother Orky was the same way.

Pete was pretty sure they had parted on good terms.

But he was also certain she and the rest of the escapees were avoiding him.

Perhaps they had some sense of the carnage they'd left behind.

The beachings off Surf Shore were only the latest.

But here, something new had been added.

If it was really true that a Great White had hit an orca calf, did that mean the shark population was reacting to the rogue pod's presence as well?

And this was a place where the sharks were there in numbers.

It also happened to host a brand-new seal colony that might attract some of the migrating transient orca pods.

That was not to mention the off-shore pods, who primarily *ate* sharks, that might be interested in the big plumply-fed Great Whites.

Of course, at least one of the big sharks off Surf Shore had bit back – albeit, an action resulting in the shark's prompt demise, but not before the pod had lost a calf – a serious trauma within orca families.

The fact that it had happened at all, suggested things were afoot that had never happened before.

You couldn't blame the animals. And you couldn't even fairly blame the randomness of nature. Too much of it went back to the meddling human hand – and *way* too much of it with the blitheness of good-intent.

Pete couldn't deny his own fingerprint. He had not intended to introduce this wild-card into an already volatile mix, but he'd been on the team that did it. That was *his* human hand.

Now, he wondered what Kate's contribution was going to be.

Pete and Tommy pulled back out of sight, watching Kate walk to her car, her sunglasses on and her hair tied up, like a celebrity advertising they didn't want to be recognized.

"What do you think she's got in mind?" Tommy asked.

Pete sighed

"Whatever it is, she thinks *big*." He shook his head. "Plus she needs funding. Cause justifies the means. She won't stop."

"I met her a while back," Tommy said. "A looker. But pure mercenary."

"Worse," Pete said, "you can buy off a mercenary. She's an idealist, convinced she's got a higher-morality. That's why she doesn't mind tapping into the Dark Side."

"Self-justifying," Tommy said.

"Maybe so," Pete said, "but she's a power that has to be respected."

He shook his head.

"And I guess, I still think she's got something genuine in her."

"Well," Tommy said, "she's a genuine *bitch*."

Pete couldn't quite disagree. But one didn't necessarily preclude the other.

Either way, whatever Kate had in mind, they were going to have to deal with her.

Pete looked out at the whale carcasses laying out on the beach, and the huge bites taken out of them, and wondered just *how* she was going to make this worse.

Reporters still milled about, and Pete saw that local fluff, Lacey Chase, had finally cornered Lauren, who was attempting to push past, with obvious impatience, even as her assistant, Nancy, blustered along behind.

The photographers were all around the whales, taking pictures of bites – especially close-ups of the *big* ones.

Without a doubt, they were some of the largest shark bites Pete had seen. And he'd been following whale carcasses down the coast for weeks.

One of those sharks had taken an orca. To Pete's knowledge, that had never happened anywhere in the world.

But if the conditions around Surf Shore were as Lauren described, what kind of situation were they looking at out there now, with the addition of his escaped rogue pod?

It seemed to Pete that they had all the elements of an ecological perfect-storm brewing.

And if he knew Kate Foster, they were all going to be running into it with a lightning rod.

CHAPTER 10

Corky had been aware for weeks that Pete was looking for her. And she was indeed steering her pack clear whenever they heard his boat approach.

They had also come to recognize the puzzling orca-like flute that lately seemed to accompany him, drifting over the air, sometimes along with some pretty good classic rock.

Truth to tell, Corky missed her human friend, but she shied away with the natural reluctance of an animal who had escaped its keeper.

It was also possible Corky understood more than that.

An orca knew, after all, what it meant to kill a human – much more than a lion, or even a dog. Corky understood that a line had been crossed at the facility.

Perhaps she even understood the concept of 'guilt by association'.

Bruno had put the association on *all* of them.

As acting big-sister of their little rag-tag, fugitive pod, and the responsibility imbued upon her, Corky's better instincts led her to steer the group clear of humans.

Still, she hadn't been able to resist hanging back on a few occasions, just to get a look at Pete's approaching boat.

Once, she had seen his shadow looking out over the water after her.

She had sensed the disapproval of the pod – they likewise understood the need to avoid humans, and Corky's lapse was worrisome. Even her normally-gregarious 'little' brother Orky seemed dour on the subject.

As a good big sister, she had led by example ever since.

That was important. Their little pod was still searching for its place in the oceanic wilderness. And nature wasn't kind to misfits.

What they had going for them was that they were all wild-born. That had been a requirement for Ryder's facility – no captive-bred individuals – those were almost all hybrids.

It also meant that Corky's pod all retained at least a memory of a natural life.

That, however, was not what they were returning to.

A person with passing knowledge might wonder why this would seem so difficult, given the well-documented intelligence and often-filmed cooperation between orcas.

But when a wild orca pod went on a hunt, it was a cohesive team, from a long-tradition of cohesive teams.

The team Corky was coaching was like taking a group of human beings, not just from random countries, customs, and languages, but random times in history.

A Spartan-warrior might not work that well with a schoolteacher from modern San Francisco.

True, they had been contained together for some time, but different eco-types tolerating each other within captive walls was one thing. Having to work together on the open ocean to survive was quite another.

But Corky was a good-sized, senior female, and she had a BIG little brother backing her up.

It also turned out Ahab was a little sweet on her.

And so, perhaps for the first time in memory – for certainly at no time in history before fifty years ago, were orcas ever captured in number, and then *certainly* never before released – individuals of different orca cultures were forced to crossover and blend.

Their little rogue pod was twelve-members deep, of at least four different eco-types.

Corky and Orky were both Puget Sound residents. Merry and Pippin were from resident pods up north near BC – all fish eaters, known for their playful nature and curiosity about humans, often filmed performing for boats. Residents were also the most common at sea-parks.

As orcas go, they were big, powerful animals, with males like Orky reaching twenty-five feet. Corky herself had attained a respectable twenty feet.

The smallest of their group was Orphan Annie, barely sixteen feet at full-maturity – a Ross Sea orca, trapped as a calf. She came from a tribe of fish-eaters, and was the smallest known killer whale species, with adult males reaching a maximum of twenty feet.

Annie was also the most traumatized and overwhelmed by the open sea. Institutionalized her entire life, she had never once hunted on her own.

An even more unlikely refugee was the Skipper, a big old North Atlantic bull. The Skipper had been in captivity for nearly thirty years, which meant he was above-average life-span for a male orca in captivity – and his body was showing all the signs, the dropping fin, his emaciated five-tons of body weight – at over twenty-six feet, he weighed more than a ton less than a healthy orca of his size and type.

Both Annie and the Skipper were basically dependent upon what the others retained of their previous wild lives.

Marty Feldman was a Subantarctic orca – named after the bizarre, and very distinct eye-patch characteristic of the type. He had been caught in a net almost ten years ago – and perhaps he retained this particular memory, because he had been pointedly teaching the others how to steal fish off of lines.

The fish-eaters in general tended towards rather frisky, frolicking behavior, often described as mischievous.

It was the mammal eaters, however, that had really earned killer whales their name.

These were the big, prehistoric barbarian warriors.

Same species as the others, but there was a different look in their eye.

Doc, Happy, and Dopey were all Pack-Ice orcas – a type known for some of the most amazing coordinated behavior ever seen in any animal – wave attacks, with three or more whales, charging in unison, sometimes swimming sideways to hide their dorsals beneath the surface, sending a surge of water over the top if ice flows, washing unsuspecting seals right off into the ocean.

Pack-ice orcas had been filmed making repeated practice runs, actually letting the seal back on the ice, so they could knock it off again and again. These attacks could be so precise that, on big flows, they would split the ice into chunks like a rack of pool balls – and like an eight-ball into the corner pocket, sending the chunk of ice carrying the seal out by itself into the open ocean.

This eco-type was also known to take whales.

The real 'whale-killer' orcas, however, were the transients.

Bruno had been a transient. And so were Ahab and Sandy.

When Bruno had gone rogue back at the facility, Ahab and Sandy had gone with him.

Neither of them had actually killed anybody, but they had helped Bruno sink a couple of boats. Responsibility for any resulting casualties was a fair case.

Wild killer whales had been known to sink boats in the past. A sailboat on a world cruise was attacked and sunk by a large male orca in 1972, stranding a father, three sons, and their small crew, into lifeboats for over three weeks.

This had been the same stretch of ocean where a rogue sperm whale had once sunk a whaling boat called *The Essex* – inspiring the novel *Moby Dick*. Naturalists have speculated that the area could be a nursery of sorts, promoting protective instincts from adults. The orcas had not pursued the human castaways, who would have been easy-pickings.

Bruno had been different that way.

Corky had known that about him all along. Just as she understood it came from the conditions that he'd lived in for ten years.

Some orcas in such environments got stuporous or catatonic. Some were known to scrape their skin and teeth away against the edges of their tanks. Some simply died.

Bruno was *angry*.

Before he'd been taken to Pete's facility, he had killed his trainer – and he had *meant* it.

Corky and Orky, along with most of the other residents, had interceded before he had added Pete and Kate Foster to his tally.

That had been their parting gift – a declaration of peace before they left the world of humans behind.

From her orca's point of view, she would have thought Pete, human might he be, would understand.

But Pete was following them.

Corky wished he would leave well enough alone.

She had become anxious just lately.

Just as when she had often been nervous back at the facility, whenever Pete would act too trustingly around Bruno, never knowing, as *she* did, the hair-trigger impulses that ruled the big bull.

For the most part, Bruno had responded to positivity. That had been the crux of Pete's rehab approach.

But in a five-ton orca, it only took a second's lapse – a second's pique.

Corky felt that tension again, only now it was all around her.

For ten years, she had visualized being back in the ocean. And for a time, living on the bay at Ryder's facility, it had been tantalizingly close.

And then one day, she had been there again. It was almost terrifying at first.

But once out on the open ocean, it was like being taken from a cage and given flight.

Yet even this blessing came with a curse.

Back out on the ocean didn't mean they were home again.

The Skipper was from the North Atlantic. Marty was a Subantarctic. They weren't getting back to their natural habitats any time soon.

Orky and Corky were Northwestern residents – and perhaps one might have thought *they*, at least, could have found their way home.

There was a catch, however. The wild pods had not experienced decadal breakdown of their cultural mores, and residents, in particular, were intolerant of transients – that they were traveling with Orky or Corky, or Merry and Pippin, made no difference.

Perhaps paradoxically, residents who were known best for their seemingly playful antics, were the most restrictively tribal in their customs and internal societies. Members never changed pods.

Transients were a little more loose – mated males would sometimes join the female's pod.

Corky, however, was in a unique situation among wild orcas.

She was pregnant – with Ahab's half-breed transient calf.

The resident pods wouldn't let her in.

That forced them out into the migratory oceanic highways.

Now they found themselves contending with the off-shore pods.

And, of course, the big transients.

Corky was aware the senior females of both of the largest pods in the area were not happy about her little ragtag group passing through.

The offshore matriarch had chased them for a few miles, a couple of weeks ago, giving up only when Corky led them sharply back towards shore.

Corky had never heard the matriarch's spoken name, but she had heard John Denver's *Calypso* played at high-volume whenever she was about. The old female was not a patient sort, and while Corky was happy to give ground, that steered them right into transient territory.

The big transient female had her tune too. Corky recognized Tommy's riff of 'My Bonnie lies over the Ocean'.

But Bonnie Parker was her pod's matriarch, and so Corky perceived her as they did – as *Mama*.

Corky had communed with her over distance. It was impossible to relate in human terms – images not of sight, but of sound, speech not with words, but with voices that traveled across the ocean like a wet-string through a paper cup.

Without ever meeting, Bonnie and Corky knew a lot about each other.

Corky knew, for example, her own group's actions had created rifts between the transients and the off-shore pods.

She also knew that Bonnie was a mother, still mourning her dead calf.

For her part, Bonnie knew that Corky was pregnant with a half-breed.

Sandy and Ahab were agitated. Both transients themselves, they recognized the imposition – the breach of decorum – that their own little rogue pod was committing across the region.

It was all very hot-button.

And in the middle of it all, Corky was going to be a mother, and there had been no one to teach her how.

Already, the odds of her calf's survival were slim.

With the presence of the transients, and the off-shore pods lurking further out, Corky's impulse as pod-leader was to quit the area. For the moment, they were outlaws, and would have to behave as such. That meant giving ground when the establishment moved in.

On the other hand, it was also a high-prey environment – and she *was* eating for two.

It was her intention to load-up as many calories as she could, and then simply continue along the migratory path, perhaps gaining days or weeks ahead, as the transients hung back around Surf Shore.

But now here Pete was, complicating things, the way humans always seemed to do.

He was putting himself in harm's way. *Again.*

She had almost gone up to him the other day, after hearing the tell-tale flute of his boat-mate. It was entrancing – like a spoken voice you could hear, but somehow not quite make out the words.

Once upon a time, Corky would have swam right up to investigate. It was a blow to the spirit that now her first instinct was to hide away.

Still, she wondered if the fact that the flute-player seemed to project, meant that he was also capable of receiving.

Corky wondered if she could actually talk back.

Her relationship with Pete had been very much one-way. She pretty much understood him. But he was only able to perceive the simplest messages and mannerisms from her.

In their way, humans were a bit retarded, especially when it came to things like empathy and perception – both orca strong-suits.

Not to mention, common sense.

Corky wished she could talk to Pete now.

If she could, she would warn him away.

This place was dangerous.

CHAPTER 11

Cody saw Lauren's number pop up on his phone and did a slow burn.

For the moment, he was content to just let it ring.

Three days he'd been in jail.

He'd kept expecting somebody to show up and vouch for him, but after what happened to Lieutenant Shaw, no one gave him a thought.

And but for a judge that had actually sat down to listen, he had been looking at six-months to a year.

The judge had been quite an attractive woman – a bit older, perhaps ten years his senior. He had reflexively given her a quick up-and-down when she'd entered the room.

She had seen the look before he caught himself.

Sitting there, in jail-clothes, unshaven for two days, Cody remembered where and who he was.

It was such a small feeling, as he realized, at the moment, he was not a man – he was a case. A person that this woman, who under other circumstances, he might offer to buy a drink, would decide if he was fit to be out among the rest of society – or perhaps needed a year-long time-out.

And just to make a good first impression, she had caught him checking out her ass.

She had smiled, seemingly bemused, shaking her head as she sat down. Cody was not sure if that was a good sign.

"Mr. Martin," she said, "my name is Judge Michelle Rosin. I called you in here, because I have been reviewing your case, and I wanted a moment with you privately, just to be sure I'm perfectly clear on the details."

She held up Cody's own hand-written statement.

"This is seriously what happened?"

Cody shrugged, nodding. He'd had about two-paragraphs worth of room. He could have gone on.

"Let me get this straight," Rosin said. "This young woman was trapped in a sunken boat, seventy-feet feet down, and you dove through shark-infested waters to pull her out?"

VERY shark-infested, Cody thought, but simply nodded.

"Yes, your honor."

The judge leaned back in her chair, laying his paperwork aside, and folding her arms.

"As near as I can tell," she said, "you're a hero. And literally the moment you got to shore, the first thing our city did was lock you up, and smear you in the press."

Cody hardly dared hope. She was repeating something he'd been muttering under his breath for two days. But he said nothing.

Judge Rosin shook her head.

"Mr. Martin, for what it's worth, I think you're a great guy. You should be getting a medal, not three days in jail. I'm going to expunge this arrest. And on behalf of this city, I'm going to apologize."

Cody had blinked. When he'd been brought aside for this little face-to-face, he'd been prepared for the worst. He hadn't even decided how he would handle it yet – whether he would be outraged and arguing, or perhaps simply plead for the next six-months of his life.

The simple kindness – simply being treated fairly, for God's sake – actually threatened to tear him up. He wiped quickly at his eye.

The judge, who seemed sharp, caught that movement too.

And so he had been released. Judge Rosin was not done with him, however, because she then did something that no one ever had before – a good deed with apparently nothing in it for herself. First, without providing details, she had made a public statement to the press announcing his complete exoneration.

The next day, there had been a visit from Kate Foster – and remarkably, Cody had found himself being offered a potentially life-changing payday.

As Kate had put it, he could use a little good publicity.

The money deal was contingent on making himself available for interviews – a couple on-camera spots for the documentary.

"I don't suppose you can act?" Kate had asked. "You could play yourself in the movie."

"Movie?" he repeated doubtfully. Rather numb at the prospect, Cody wondered how that would play as advertising next to his on-line mugshot – run front-page on the local rag *again.*

"I'm camera shy," he told her.

"A shame," Kate said, "you have a good smile."

She had given him her own smile then, and Cody could see she knew how to smile at men. He could at least stop worrying he was being manipulated and simply assume it as a given.

Kate also told him the filmmakers wanted to film the docudrama on the site where it happened. For authenticity.

"I can't properly express," Cody had said, "how dangerously stupid that would be."

He, however, would be happy to sign on the dotted line, and stay on shore while they ran along ahead.

Did that mean he was selling out? Or did it mean he'd finally gotten a little luck?

He supposed, if he *wanted* to, he could look upon it as a reward. Judge Rosin had clearly intended this as, not just reputation-restoration, but a windfall. Hell, it would seem ungrateful, not to mention downright foolish, to turn away – like tearing up a winning lottery ticket.

Of course, as Lauren's number rang again, he could guess at least one woman he knew wouldn't think so.

But there was nothing that said he had to answer the phone.

He shut the ringer off, quite satisfied *that* was one conversation he wouldn't miss.

After a moment, there was a knock at the door.

Cody's eyes narrowed, his breath letting loose in a slow burn.

Resigned, he went to the door and opened it.

Lauren stood on his porch, her phone still in her hand.

"Hello, Cody," she said. "I heard your phone ringing. You didn't answer."

"That's kind of answer enough, isn't it?"

"It's kind of chicken-shit."

"Now *that*," Cody said, "is a hell of a thing to say to me."

Letting his temper rise, he started to close the door. For a second, he thought it would be that easy.

"Wait!"

Lauren blocked the doorjamb, inserting her body. For the tiniest moment, Cody was tempted to just shove her out on the porch.

He supposed it boiled down to how much trouble he was willing to go to in order to avoid whatever trouble she planned to bring in with her.

It was a toss-up.

For the moment, he left her pinned in the doorjamb.

"What do you want, Lauren?"

"Please," she said, pushing the door back open and letting herself into his apartment. "Listen. I just want to talk."

She looked around at his place, her first time in his inner-sanctum.

Her wrinkled nose said enough.

Cody scraped a living as a scuba-instructor and part-time general-laborer, and his accommodations showed it.

Lauren's father owned a hotel chain. Her camping trips weren't *this* rough.

She panned the room slowly, as if for a place to sit, but then chose to simply stand. She turned to him with an accusatory eye.

"I can't believe you took money," she said.

Cody chirped a brief laugh.

"Are you kidding? What am I supposed to do? I'm sorry if it gives your sharks bad press."

His temper ticked another notch.

"I've gotta eat, don't I? I'm kind of hard to hire with all these arrests for assault. Thanks for leaving me there to *rot*, by the way."

That backed her on her heels, and she looked a bit shamed.

"I'm sorry. I meant to explain..."

She shrugged helplessly.

"I was actually mad at *you*, for not visiting me in the hospital."

Cody looked back at her, stunned.

"Well," he said, "I woulda."

They both stood silent for a moment.

Funny how they so quickly jumped to a lot of the wrong conclusions about each other.

Everyone said Lauren *looked* just like Carson – in the *Sharks and Babes* videos, everyone assumed they were sisters, maybe twins. But ironically, Lauren was more like Cody – she was the sensible-sister. Cody had been the leash on the wildcat.

To a certain extent, they both felt like they'd failed their jobs.

They also knew they were both eager to blame the other for it.

"Listen," Cody said, finally, "if this is about the contract, I'm sorry, I already signed it."

He threw up his hands. "Come on. It would be stupid not to. It's Hollywood money. So they make a movie? What's the harm?"

"This was yesterday? I guess you didn't hear what she's added to the menu."

Lauren had her hands on her hips, and her head cocked as she spoke. Cody was surprised to see she was actually struggling with her own temper.

"What if I told you she's planning on towing all those beached whales out to sea, and selling tickets to watch sharks eat them?"

"Well," Cody said, nodding slowly. "I'd say, that's a pretty bad idea."

"Well, she's doing it. Thanks to you."

"Uhhhh, *no*," Cody corrected. "She's doing a documentary and a movie because of me." He shook his head. "Don't hang anything else she does on my back."

"You admit it's dangerous?"

"Well, Hell-*yeah*. *I'm* sure not going out there. I'm not going bungee-jumping either. And I can't see jumping out of a perfectly good airplane just for fun."

"Meaning," Lauren said, eyeing him levelly, "that you won't do anything to stop it?"

"Why would I?"

"It's exploitive," Lauren said. "It's everything Carson would have hated."

Cody's eyes simmered. Always right to the low-blow. Bringing *her* up?

It ruined the brief moment he'd thought they were having.

"Yeah," Cody said. "She and I used to fight about *just* that kind of thing."

He was still standing by the door, and now he stepped aside and pulled it open again.

"By the way," he said, "you don't get to use that anymore. If a few people would have listened to me all along, there'd be a few less dead people. And Carson was one of them."

He swung the door wide, giving her the exit.

"Lauren, will you just please leave me alone?"

Lauren hung a moment longer. Their blood was up. If she stayed, they were going to have a real fight. Although to be fair, it wasn't like they'd started out friends.

Cody resisted the urge, even though his teeth were already primed.

Part of it was that she was *right*, of course. Carson *would* have been utterly outraged.

On the other hand, Carson had also dumped him. And he wasn't kidding about needing money. As he saw it, his choices were continuing to live in ever-progressive destitution, or accept a near-miraculous windfall.

That part didn't seem real yet, and he still didn't quite trust it.

It was money, yet to be made. What his mother would have called pie-in-the-sky.

Still, it was a shot at something better. And maybe Carson would have wanted *that* for him.

And as far as Lauren?

Well, if he owed her anything, he thought he had it covered by fishing her out of a sunken charter boat, goddammit. She'd cracked a wrist in the incident – *he'd* had his ribs set in the jailhouse infirmary.

If it was time to have *that* fight, then it was time.

But Lauren turned away, pushing past him without another word. She didn't look back on her way to her car.

Cody shut the door and sat down.

His mood was soured. There had been a moment, just for a second, when part of him had been happy to see her.

He wondered about that – just as he wondered what had pushed him out of a boat after her, right among circling Great Whites.

It actually hadn't been as suicidal as it sounded. He'd planned ahead with several canisters of shark-repellent – a *scent-of-death* extract created from dead shark tissue, it was a remarkably effective deterrent that caused sharks of the same species to scatter.

Unfortunately, he'd had a finite supply, and the currents washed the chemicals away very quickly.

So, it had still been a pretty hairy dive.

And theoretically, Cody *hated* Lauren – his ex's evil best-friend. And Lauren, for her part, utterly detested him.

Yet, she had blasted Big Rhonda with a spear-gun, right when Cody was about to get his own ass bit off.

He couldn't say she hadn't helped.

There wasn't a psychological-mechanism in Cody's entire personality that would have allowed today's confrontation to go any other way, but he found himself wishing it hadn't.

Was it still about Carson? Just wanting her family, her best-friend, to like him?

If that was it, he decided he would much rather not care.

That was when another knock came from the door.

Cody sighed.

Was she really coming back?

And did it mean they were going to have their fight after all? He could picture her sitting out in her car, steaming, before finally marching back up the walk.

Setting his teeth, Cody got up and answered the door.

But it wasn't Lauren. A man stood at the door, approximately Kate's age, but dressed in the rumpled gear of the life-long beach-bum – minus the year-round-tan of the Southern California surfer-crowd.

"Cody Martin?" the man said, extending his hand. "My name is Tommy Larson. And I understand you've got white sharks killing orcas 'round these parts."

CHAPTER 12

Doby had been hovering near shore for the past twenty-four hours. He had mostly stayed low, not far off the beach.

There was human activity all over – helicopters, boats.

And, of course, people milling on the beach like ants, surrounding the beached bodies, not only of Berta and her pod, but a whole troop of big baleens.

Doby's wounds were still smarting but, so far, the rogue orcas had not reappeared. It seemed they were avoiding humans too.

The big cachalot knew he should quit the area. He understood in his own way, what had happened to Berta and the others, and that they were not coming back.

Something held him there all the same. He was an old whale, set in his ways, perhaps having a hard time accepting the change.

Still, there was nothing to be gained remaining around humans, seeing them crawl, bug-like, over the carcasses that lay rotting on shore.

He knew the orcas were still prowling the coast. Even over distance, Doby detected their odd echoing sonar ping.

The transient killer whale pods were also coming in close this year. And while they were typically after seals, they *were* mammal-eaters. True, they had rarely been known to bother a cachalot – at least not a big male like Doby.

But who knew? This rogue pod certainly had. And Doby had seen the transient pods taking other big whales – even giant blues.

And Doby needed no doctorate to understand that the sheer number of sharks was also likely to bring in the big, off-shore shark-eater pods.

Except, waiting for *them* were BIG sharks, who were learning to bite back.

All around him, the sounds of the sea echoed ever more shrill.

Berta's was not the only pod of cachalots to be hit along the coast. Besides the mass beachings of the easily-frightened baleens, Doby had encountered fleeing stragglers from another group of sperm whales – a pod, whose senior female, the Lotharion Doby had mated with *last* season – a trio of adolescent males, ripped and scarred with fresh, bleeding wounds.

The young whales were just at the crest of being old enough to venture out on their own, abandoning the tropical nurseries to join the senior bulls in their solitary existence up north.

But now that leap had been made for them. Doby could hear them, injured and frightened, as they had meandered along the coast, inexpertly trying to navigate the northern migration route, sending wide-open and obvious sonar, bouncing off the canyons like falling rocks, scaring off food, as they dived deep.

Yesterday, Doby had tried to approach them – not aggressively – possibly just looking for the company of his own kind – but the group of them had fled, scattering like so much bait-fish, any illusions of being top predator a fast-fading memory.

To be fair, Doby could relate.

He knew he should leave with them – and quickly. His every instinct told him it was time to quit this coast – to lick his wounds and simply get on with the business of survival, as he had done for nearly eighty years.

Yet, still he lingered.

Grief? Attachment? How much of these things Doby experienced, no one could truly say.

But for whatever reason, Doby remained, skulking just out of sight.

CHAPTER 13

Lauren called Pete about Kate's plan the moment she left Cody's place.

"'*Great White Feeding Frenzy*'," Pete repeated back. "You gotta love her."

He asked Lauren to meet at the little restaurant on the docks by his motel.

She knew the place, small and innocuous, called 'The Fish Shack', and it had the freshest, right-out-of-the-ocean seafood, with the biggest crabs and shellfish. It was a recent discovery of Lauren's – and a long-time secret pleasure of Carson's, because any good activist knew that the seafood-industry was depleting the ocean.

Cody had taken her there on the day of Carson's funeral. It had been his and Carson's special spot.

Lauren had inadvertently discovered it also served some pretty stiff drinks. She had over-indulged on oyster-shooters, and Cody had been obliged to carry her home.

She shut her eyes, hoping the waitress wouldn't recognize her, but agreed to meet Pete for lunch.

Annie, the waitress, was talking to Pete at his booth – seemingly with interest – and her face did indeed spark with recognition when Lauren walked in.

Pete waved her over. Lauren made polite eye-contact with Annie as she slid into the booth, catching Annie's raised brow as she did so.

Lauren sighed. Last time, she'd been carried out drunk. Today, she was here with another guy – an older guy, no less.

With a look that suggested she was *narrowly* choosing discretion, Annie tapped her menu-pad. "Give you a minute, honey?"

"Please," Lauren said.

Annie stepped away, shaking her head.

Pete caught the exchange, but didn't ask.

"Thanks for coming," he offered, smiling.

It was a good smile. She found she still instinctively liked him, and appropriately girded herself to remain stiff and suspicious.

"So," he said, "how'd you get along with Kate Foster?"

Lauren could see he already knew the answer. Anticipating her mood, she thought, just like a trainer.

"I can't say I quite trusted her," she said.

Pete nodded.

"I'm glad you've got good judgment."

"What she's got in mind... it's..."

"Stirring up a lotta shit," Pete finished. "Yeah. That's what she does. She's a veteran shit-stirrer."

"She's deliberately starting a major feeding frenzy," Lauren replied, a little irritated at his flip-tone, "specifically involving multiple endangered species, in an ecologically imbalanced area."

"Yep. A *lotta* shit," Pete agreed. "You get used to it. You've gotta hand it to her. She can't *just* tow those whales out to sea." He shook his head. "No. Kate thinks exponentially."

"And," he said, "she *always* thinks she's in control."

He tapped his cane against his battered leg.

"That's the point where things start getting dangerous."

Pete eyed Lauren seriously.

"And it *is* dangerous out there, isn't it, Doctor?"

Lauren nodded slowly.

"There are more sharks than I've ever seen," she said. "Big adults. From at least two, normally separated populations, all coming together."

"And one of them hit an orca," Pete said. "Along with a gray whale calf."

Lauren nodded.

"I suppose," she ventured, "considering it's a space and numbers problem, Kate's idea *might* draw some of them away."

"Thirty whales towed out all at once? Pretty invasive, wouldn't you say?"

"At least it's non-lethal."

Pete paused on the remark, eyeing her thoughtfully.

"Why does it have to be non-lethal?" he asked.

Lauren's lip curled, almost imperceptibly, not quite covering an easily-touched nerve.

There it was.

"Seriously," Pete continued, "if it's a population problem, why not just have a fishing season? Cull the numbers down a little?"

He stopped, seeing the look in her eye.

"What?" he said. "They're just fish."

"So you just want to kill them all?" Lauren felt the automatic tick in her blood-pressure. This subject was always a sure-bet to piss her off.

Pete could tell.

"I didn't say kill them *all*, did I? Seriously, people pull millions of fish out of the ocean every day, just for food. There's nothing wrong with a responsible haul, to bring down numbers of dangerous species."

"Suppose someone wanted to kill your precious orcas?" Lauren asked, her temper pulling at its leash.

"Orcas," he replied, "aren't just fish."

Pete held up his hands, as if to apologize for the facts.

"I'm sorry," he said. "Look, I don't romanticize or anthropomorphize, but there *is* a difference."

He held up the menu. "You eat fish, don't you?"

Lauren didn't answer. She actually hadn't ordered yet. For a moment, she let herself be angry, because *now* she wasn't going to – just to make a point.

"Over-fishing," Lauren said, as if she'd never given the tantalizing menu a thought, "is depleting the ocean. No one should eat fish."

"But not because you empathize with the fish," Pete said.

He stopped, gauging her, obviously seeing her hackles were up. This was where she expected him to simply capitulate – to start working the superficial charm.

Instead, he leaned forward.

"Bottom line," he said, "I get that you love sharks. And I'm not criticizing you for that. Not at all. But no matter how much you love them, no matter how magnificent they are, a Great White shark isn't ever going to be your friend."

He leaned back.

"When Corky and the rest of them escaped, I lost all my friends."

"I thought you didn't anthropomorphize."

"I don't. Ever had a dog, Doctor?"

He met her challenging eye.

"Don't you see?" he said. "This is personal for me. I've been trying to keep tabs, long distance, but they stay away from humans now. They're unique in the ocean. An anomaly. Shunned by their own kind."

"And," Pete added, "I think Corky's pregnant. With a half-breed."

He sighed.

"I think that's why they're traveling together like they are. And why they left the Northwest. A resident pod won't accept a transient. Resident females have attacked transient males in captivity. Corky would be unwelcome with a hybrid-calf. They would likely either drive them out or kill them."

"So why are they following the migration routes?" Lauren asked. "Just to hunt whales?"

"Possibly," Pete said. "On the other hand, the transient-pods are looser. They're wilder, more dangerous. But their group coercion isn't as tight. Males will sometimes join other transient pods after mating."

"Is that what you're hoping for?"

"I don't know." Pete sighed, looking out the window towards the ocean.

"They're doing a hell of a lot of damage out there," he said. "Orcas are super-predators who have cultivated their hunting grounds for thousands of years. This little group, by itself, is disrupting all that.

"I suppose," he said, "if Corky and her group started traveling with a transient-pod, they might start behaving according to *their* culture."

"It sounds," Lauren said, "like you're being a bit invasive yourself, Doctor Nichols."

"Possibly," Pete said. "But don't put me in a position of defending something I don't believe. The whole point of our rehab facility was *not* to just turn them loose in the wild. And I can't even blame it on the activists – although they did their damned, bloody best. The orcas took care of it themselves."

Now he looked at her seriously.

"You asked me how I'd feel, if someone wanted to kill my 'precious orcas'? I've got a feeling that, if they keep behaving as they are, that's exactly what's going to happen. The public loves orcas, but a few more images like *this*..."

He held up his phone, showing a video of Surf Shore's beaches, littered with giant rotting corpses.

Now for the first time, his gregarious features darkened.

"The public loves orcas. But much more of this and the bleeding-hearts will turn on them. It's easy enough to justify. They aren't like wild orcas, after all. They've been tainted by *humans*."

There was bitterness in his voice. Worse, a frustrated anger.

Lauren heard it, and found herself wondering if he was really on her side in any of this.

She had caught the reference to 'bleeding hearts'. That was code-speak of the enemy.

Lauren looked at him appraisingly.

"You really don't like people like me, do you?" she said.

He looked right back at her.

"Actually," he said, "I very *much* like people like you. I admire your brains, your courage, and most of all, your passion." He shrugged. "I just find that people like you don't much like *me*."

He eyed her knowingly.

"A dreamer doesn't like a realist. But a realist loves a dreamer."

He smiled.

"I guess that's why I'm still single."

But Lauren wasn't about to be charmed. She pushed away from the table and stood.

"I'm going to the mayor's office tomorrow," she said, "and I'm going to try and get him to block this whole operation. I don't suppose you'd care to come with me?"

"I doubt my testimony would carry much weight. I've got legal troubles of my own. And if you think talking to the mayor of this little burg is going to make the slightest difference, you are dramatically underestimating Kate Foster."

"Will you come?"

"I've got plans."

"This is dangerous what's going on."

"No argument there."

"And you're going to let it happen. What if someone gets hurt?"

"I'm not *letting* anything happen. I think you're dramatically *over-*estimating me."

Lauren eyed him coldly.

"Apparently," she said.

Pete frowned. It was a low-blow and she could tell it hurt a bit. But when he replied, his voice was tired, not angry.

"Right there," he said. "See? That's the dreamer in you. Don't ever lose it. For what it's worth, I wish you luck."

Lauren turned to leave, just as Annie came walking back with her note-pad. Lauren took the opportunity to push past her, avoiding any further awkwardness, as she left The Fish Shack for the first time on her own two feet.

Sitting in his booth alone, Pete watched her go. Then he turned to the window, looking towards the ocean.

"Damn," he whispered. "*Damn.*"

CHAPTER 14

Cody had heard of Tommy Larson.

He'd seen the on-line videos – Tommy had been a fixture in the Northwest since he was a kid. Someone had even done a montage – a lot of distance photos, taken by others – a kid out on a kayak, surrounded by six-foot towering orca fins, often seen playing on a flute. As he'd grown older, he'd taken out on the open ocean, filming his own interactions with the big transient pods – one of the largest eco-types, with adult males sometimes approaching eight tons.

Known to take down hundred-foot blue whales, these wild, dinosaur-sized alpha-predators seemed to accept Tommy and his small boat as easily as one of their own. More than that, breaching and showing off, as if for a preferred guest.

It was the sort of thing Cody had dismissed as on-camera stunts, not all that different from what Carson and Lauren had been doing with sharks.

But there *was* a subtle difference. Tommy Larson's legend sprouted spontaneously around him. It wasn't something he'd posted on the Internet, to gain money or fame.

Cody knew his basic history – orphaned, raised by his aunt after his parents had died in a boat wreck on Puget Sound, swamped in an unexpected squall. Tommy himself had been twelve-years old, and had been found washed ashore.

Purportedly, when rescuers had found him, shivering and cold, there had been a pod of orcas circling offshore.

The legend, of course, was that the orcas had rescued him. At the time, Tommy claimed not to remember. And when he'd grown older, he'd dismissed the tale as just a story that got started.

Although, that *had* been when he'd first started venturing out on the water.

Now that he'd met him, Cody found himself wondering if the story were true. You heard of dolphins rescuing shipwreck survivors – even protecting them from sharks. And an orca was basically a big dolphin.

When Tommy showed up at his door yesterday, it had seemed impolite to ask – like asking a celebrity about their divorce you saw in the tabloids.

But now, out on the water with him, he saw a sort of focused acuity with the ocean that made him think of some of the old surfing gurus he'd met in Hawaii.

Cody considered himself fairly savvy on the water, but Tommy rode the ocean like a skipping rock.

He had met Tommy and Doctor Nichols – who introduced himself as 'Pete' – at the same dock where he'd been arrested just a few days before. His own boat was still impounded. The dock foreman, who he'd bowled over on the way out to rescue Lauren, glared at him from his office.

Tommy had a nice-sized outboard – a pretty tricked-out vessel, in fact, with blinking computer screens and studio-level stereo equipment. It was just large enough to house a lower cabin with bunks.

"This has been home the last few weeks," Pete said.

"Better than *my* place," Cody remarked.

Tommy fired up the engine. It sounded as smooth as a purring cat – a *big* cat.

But it *was*, Cody noted unhappily, smaller than the charter boat Big Rhonda had taken out.

And now, here they were, on their way right out to the very same spot.

Cody settled in, resigned, letting the wind cut at his hair.

"Would you recognize the orca pod that took out that shark?" Pete asked.

Cody shrugged. "Nothing specific other than they were orcas. And the one that took out Rhonda was a female."

"Any drooping fins among them?"

"Not that I saw."

Tommy and Pete exchanged looks.

"Definitely a wild pod," Tommy said.

"After the shark had killed its calf," Pete agreed. "Not a predatory attack."

"Maybe one of the transients," Tommy said. "Bonnie's passing through this time of year."

Tommy pulled them away from the docks, heading out over the drop-off into deep water, before veering sharply south.

"There's usually two types of orca that you see around here," he said. "The offshore-pods can range all the way from California to Alaska. They're shark-eaters."

"Now they don't *normally* feed on Great Whites," Tommy cautioned, "because those are sharks that mostly hunt near shore. The shark-eater orcas don't come in that close, because the open ocean is where the largest populations of sharks are. Not the scattered Great Whites along the coast. They have to go where there's biomass."

"Except," Cody said, "there's a little extra bio-mass off Surf Shore these days."

Tommy and Pete both nodded.

"Yeah," Pete said. "That had occurred to us."

"The off-shore pods also travel in large groups," Tommy said. "Sometimes two-hundred or more. And they're a smaller eco-type. Typically, adult males are under seven meters."

"The pod I saw had animals in it a lot bigger than seven meters," Cody said. "And there was maybe twenty of them."

Pete nodded.

"Transients. Eight-meter-plus. And they're husky."

"And they also range the Pacific coast," Tommy said.

The boat was now cresting the peninsula.

"Just around the bend," Cody directed. "The rocks break the wind into a little cove."

"That's the seal colony?" Pete pulled out his binoculars.

Sure enough, they already could hear the traffic-like honking of elephant seals on the distant rocks. The sound carried on the wind.

"Yep," Pete said, focusing. "There they are."

Even in the distance, the modest beach was visibly milling with elephant seals.

"That might have brought Bonnie's pod in, alright" Tommy said. He looked out at the empty ocean. "I wonder if they're still around."

He hit the stereo and *Quadrophenia* broadcasted out into the surrounding water.

Out on the ocean, the acoustics were as clear as a concert hall. Cody actually felt himself drifting with the music.

"Bonnie likes this one," Tommy said.

"It's a good one," Cody agreed.

"Residents prefer Bob Marley," Pete remarked.

After *The Who* song finished, Tommy put on *Zeppelin*.

"Let me get this straight," Cody said. "You get paid to sit out here on the ocean, play records, blow your flute, and trip on killer whales?"

"He really does," Pete said. "Ain't that a *bitch*?"

"Actually," Tommy replied easily, "it really isn't about the money. All this is free. *And* so is my room and board. So any money I actually *do* make just goes into savings."

Tommy considered.

"And booze and women," he said. "I do get to shore from time to time."

Pete smirked. He happened to know Tommy had actually taken dates out on the water to *meet* the whales. Tommy, with all due discretion and no names, had shaken his head and simply repeated, "*Aphrodisiac*."

Cody marveled.

"Clearly, I've been doing something wrong," he said.

Tommy changed the record again, this time putting in some hip-hop.

"This sometimes gets their attention," he said.

But now, he was frowning, because the ocean surface revealed nothing.

No, Cody thought, as movement in the waves caught his eye – not nothing.

A slim dorsal fin broke the surface. But not an orca.

It was the short, triangular dorsal of a shark, slicing through the water like a knife.

"I guess he likes the beats," Cody said.

Tommy nodded. "Sharks are attracted to vibrations."

After a moment's consideration, Tommy reached over and turned the speakers off.

The fin cruised easily by and they could clearly see the massive shape gliding just below the surface.

"That's a damn big shark," Pete said respectfully. "Eighteen or nineteen feet."

"I'm telling you," Cody said, "that's been average this year. And there's a *lot* of them."

"And one of them took out your friend's boat," Pete said, eyeing the massive fish, even as it turned, circling.

Tommy raised his hand and pointed. A second and third fin had appeared. Now that the first had broken the surface, the others were emboldened.

Great Whites were actually kind of skittish. They spent a lot of time working up their nerve before they attacked. They often stalked prey for an extended stretch.

You never knew they were there.

The second and third fin were every bit as large as the first. And in the manner of sharks, they circled, edging ever closer.

Natural behavior, but today it felt wrong. It felt actively *predatory*.

Cody kept his expression mild, unconcerned

"Kind of spooky out here," he remarked casually.

Tommy glanced at Pete.

"He's not wrong," he said.

"They're posturing," Pete said, indicating the circling fins. "Doctor Palmer was right. The congestion has got them aggressive and territorial."

"And I'll bet the presence of orcas has them on hair-trigger," Tommy said.

Cody eyed the circling fins, wondering how many more might still be lurking down below, out of sight.

Probably a lot.

"Maybe," he said, "we should get a bigger boat."

Tommy regarded the fins, compared to his rather modest, if well-tricked-out water-craft.

He gunned the throttle, turning the boat back north.

"You know," he said, "that might not be such a bad idea."

With a deliberate and perhaps self-conscious wake, Tommy angled them back out towards the peninsula.

Nether Tommy or Pete spoke on the way back, and they both seemed pensive. Cody was no scientist, but he could tell they hadn't liked what they'd seen.

He patted the unruly hairs down on the back of his own neck as they left the cove behind.

Behind them, in the empty, vacated backwash of their wake, yet another fin appeared, larger than all the rest.

It rose up quietly, even as the boat sped away.

Bloody Mary cruised the surface briefly, her acute senses registering the departing boat.

Around her, the other sharks gave respectful distance.

After a moment, Mary dropped back down into the deep darkness and out of sight.

CHAPTER 15

Bonnie Parker had known her human name for a long time. She even knew how to say it in her language. There were recorded images of Bonnie herself squeaking out an imitation of 'My Bonnie lies over the Ocean'.

It sounded better underwater.

She generally avoided humans, having learned early on that one friendly human didn't mean the next one was. The nick in her dorsal fin, courtesy of a harpoon, had been given to her as a calf.

Besides, mixing with humans was something *residents* did. Transient pods were more aloof.

A little more woodsy-wild.

On the other hand, so was the oddball human who had given Bonnie her name.

She knew he was called Tommy, but had no way to say it.

Bonnie had recognized the sound of his flute, a sound that greeted her every year during her seasonal migration through the Northwestern waters, but she had never encountered him this far south.

Naturally curious animals, such things required investigation.

When Bonnie had first heard Tommy's bumping stereo, playing all her greatest-hits, she had turned the pod in that direction.

But then he had started playing recordings of what Bonnie perceived as the 'others' – the rogue pod that had been shadowing them down the coast, holding a deliberate, tangent distance, making sure never to cross paths.

Bonnie had stopped short of Tommy's boat.

It grew worse a moment later, when he pulled out his flute, normally a pleasant, if incoherent, vocalization.

But on this day, the flute squawked notes reminiscent of the rogues.

Bonnie faded back, pulling her pod with her.

Over the following days, they had trailed Tommy and Pete down the coast, staying out of sight, often several miles distant, yet still tracking their boat as they made their way south. Bonnie didn't know what Tommy's relation was to the rogues, but they clearly seemed to be following them.

At this point, Bonnie was too. Their presence was becoming a problem.

For one thing, by taking different types of prey, they were stepping on toes. Feathers were ruffling that were unaccustomed to being ruffled.

There had already been a brief skirmish between a couple of members of her pod, and one of the big off-shore pods. No orcas had actually been killed, but it was the first orca-on-orca fight in Bonnie's lifetime. There was not even a cultural memory of such things.

Bonnie knew the off-shore matriarch well – the one Tommy called Calypso – and she was known to hold a grudge. The pod of rogues was picking fights that Bonnie didn't want.

One could also reasonably make a case that this marauding band of misfit orcas had dramatically worsened the situation at Surf Shore. They had driven this season's Great Whites out of the Farallons and into these waters. You could logically draw a direct connection to the increased shark activity and aggression.

And by extension, why Bonnie's calf had been taken.

Bonnie remembered, to the moment, what it had been like when she had appeared with her pod, to discover Big Rhonda guarding the floating carcass of her calf – as if it were *her* piece of meat.

Rhonda was nearly as large as Great Whites get – over twenty feet and two-and-a-half tons. But Bonnie was a transient-matriarch – almost twenty-two feet at three-and-a-half tons, and she had been leading her pod for thirty years.

What this shark had done... to take her calf...?

Orca societies were built around mothers and their calves. Pods were females with their adult children. The big males, some over thirty feet long and nine-tons, the most dominant large predator in the history of the ocean, were basically a bunch of mama's boys.

Mothers separated from calves in captivity had been known to call out for weeks.

Bonnie's initial reaction, however, at the slaughter of her young, was pure rage.

If this shark wanted to move up into the whale-leagues, *this* was how she handled whales.

Bonnie had hit Big Rhonda hard enough to knock her nearly twenty-feet out of the water – much as Rhonda herself had been filmed doing to many a hapless seal.

Then Bonnie and her pod had torn the big shark apart. They had shared the liver.

But that had done little to allay her grief. As a mother, the loss of her calf was fresh.

No one could say if Bonnie's mind really worked this way, but it was also possible she connected the dots to the rogue pod.

Bonnie was aware of the 'other' – the 'big sister'. Bonnie had heard her name spoken as well – the humans called her Corky.

For weeks, her pod's jailhouse squeaks and clicks bounced off the walls of the continental shelf.

Bonnie had also heard the more baritone, bellowing calls of the big baleens, as the rogue pod chased down one after the other.

Then there were the cachalots.

Doby, Bonnie knew, had been injured. His females butchered.

If he lived, he would be laying for orcas – a cachalot never forgot.

But there was a final atrocity, worse than all the rest.

Corky was pregnant. With a hybrid.

Bonnie could not quantify her outrage – not in a way a person could understand. It was a violation of decorum. It... *offended* her. Things were being done that were not to be done.

A delicate balance was being upset.

And as it always seemed it must be, it would all be resolved by conflict.

When push came to shove, that was always the final solution, and it would be here.

Bonnie had brought her own pod in close this year. It was her intention to find Corky and her refugees, and drive them out of the region – out of the North Pacific entirely. They simply couldn't be tolerated.

So far, however, the rogues had evaded them.

CHAPTER 16

Kate had just gotten off the phone with Surf Shore's mayor. Lauren had been in to try and warn him off.

The mayor, a local businessman named Kirby, who owned motels, had gotten the job to streamline the tourist trade, and was already not happy with Lauren's previous recommendation that they shut down all their surfing revenue.

Kate understood politics. She also recognized that she was bringing in Hollywood money, nearly on the heels of the town's primary income source being cut-off. Therefore, she knew Kirby's decision as far as tomorrow's operation was already made.

The tug boats were already arranged. A film crew was meeting them at the docks first thing in the morning.

Kate had even brought the hastily-assembled cast, set for the docudrama. They would use the promotion to introduce the actors, and then splice them with backgrounds and interviews of the actual players – all being scripted at that very moment.

They had thirty dead whales that they were towing out past the drop-off, with two sixty-five-foot tugs set to do the grunt work.

More impressively, the studio had provided a fancy tour-boat – usually based in Hawaii, it was designed to cater events and parties, and sported a transparent poly-carbonate window in the hull, for an underwater viewing port.

This was where the bulk of the on-site live-stream would be broadcast. The actors would be on-board and allowed to interact with the VIP guests.

"Feeding Frenzy' was up to a million likes within a half-hour after Kate first put the ad up this morning.

It was almost amusing that Lauren thought she was going to derail all that.

Kate had just been getting out of the tiny motel shower, and its finite supply of lukewarm water, when Mayor Kirby had called.

Tying up her hair, pulling her robe over her shivering skin, she was already a little irritated. Still she knew the hoops.

Mayor Kirby dutifully voiced Lauren's list of concerns, most of which were allayed by Kate's assurance that every participant would be signing a liability waiver.

When the mayor told her that Lauren had threatened to go to the press, Kate laughed.

"We've already arranged for a local news-chopper. David Templeton's network purchased the rights to the live-feed. Trust me, we'd *love* to have her on camera. We'll splice it with her background story, and interview the actress playing her.

"And," she added, "if she's worried about getting sunk, tell her we're getting a *lot* bigger boat. In fact, if the press asks, *say* that."

Reassured, Mayor Kirby had laughed and thanked her. Kate was just shutting off her phone when it rang again.

This time when she saw the number, she frowned.

Doctor Lauren Phillips was not a problem. It was unfortunate that she had decided to be an obstacle, but for Kate, that meant she was just a different sort of useful prop. Lauren was still a *girl* – idealistic in all the wrong ways.

Still, she had time to learn. Once this was over, Kate would be able to show her how you got results.

As Pete had once said to her, "Cause doesn't justify means. Results do."

Of course, he had also said, "You just have to be honest about your results."

Lauren wasn't a problem.

Pete, on the other hand...

She looked at his number. She had purposely never assigned him a ringtone.

Kate let the phone ring. The first rule in combat – don't let the enemy engage until you are ready.

If Pete had something that might derail the project, it was best that the project already be underway. Pete could expect Kate to be hard to reach until around mid-day tomorrow.

She set her phone down as it finally stopped ringing.

Then there was a knock at the door.

Kate cursed under her breath.

She considered simply not answering.

But he would wait all night. The sonofabitch was stubborn.

When she opened the door, Pete was holding up his room key.

"It's a small town," he said. "There aren't that many motels. I'm only two doors down."

He nodded at the tiny little room behind her.

"Looks like you're slumming it these days," he said. "Must be quite a come-down. Personally, I'm just glad not to be sleeping on-board that damn boat."

"What do you want, Pete?" Kate said, warily. "I told you my lawyers said we shouldn't speak."

"You *did* say that," he replied, for the record, as he measured her with those damned earnest eyes.

For just a moment, she thought he was going to make a pass.

Instead, he fired a shot across her bow.

"Going for Hollywood money this time? Need a new sponsor?"

Kate cocked her head, locking horns, right in the middle.

"I already had Hollywood money," she said. "I'm just spreading it around. That's what I do."

She folded her arms challengingly, even as she tried to read his face.

Pete's crooked smile was his natural expression – the face he wore on his boat, when he was braced against the wind, squinting into the sun.

He was braced like that today. It wasn't him angry, really, but it was the sort of face Kate imagined he wore in a fight. Alert, but purposeful – and very, very serious.

"Honestly, Kate," he said, "do you have to exploit *everything*?"

And with that, he smacked his cane on the floor – hard.

Kate blinked. That was when she realized he really *was* angry after all.

He shut his eyes, taking a breath. Kate had seen that before too – Doctor Pete controlling his temper and making his dutiful attempt to *reason* with her.

"Kate," he said, "you are deliberately triggering an ecological event in a high-risk area."

"Sharks eat whales all the time."

"Not more than two-dozen large baleens in the same *Great White*-infested area at once. And then for-God's-sake putting *people* out there?"

But seeing her face, Pete stopped short. Kate wondered if he might finally be learning the lesson of futility, and stop challenging her on every damned thing.

That was not the case.

Twice tonight, she'd been wrong about him. He wasn't appealing to her reason. He had been making a statement of justification.

"We both know," he said, "Agnes Walker, Washington state's ambitious new Attorney General, is interested in making a name for herself. I've also been informed that my testimony regarding the death of Maggie Kirkland and her little group of eco-activists outside the rehab facility that night, is likely going to be subpoenaed."

Kate's brows raised, surprised that he would go there.

She didn't buy it for a second, of course. Extorting her against something he might say to the AG's office? Nope. He was too nice a guy.

Despite his sell-out, working-for-the-dark-side, life-choices, he was scrupulously honest within his own code.

Pete Nichols was not the type to bluff, let alone extort.

He shook his head sadly.

"If you're thinking that I can't bluff, you're right. Kate... I'm *pleading* with you. Don't *do* this. I was out there today. Something's wrong with this place. It's... it isn't safe."

He looked at her with those damned earnest eyes again.

"I'm saying I'm worried," he said, helplessly. "Personally. For *you*."

That one actually set her back.

Kate was consistently irritated by the male protective instinct, but recognized it as empirical reality, and therefore always used it to her benefit. Now, it was potentially an element that might actually work against her.

If Pete thought he was *protecting* her, might he not take drastic steps?

She eyed him carefully.

Nope, she decided. She had his number.

"You do what you have to do," she said.

Kate stood there, her robe slightly, deliberately ajar, with just the loosest knot tied across her waste – dripping-wet, and goosebump-naked underneath. She had found it was a good position to argue with men.

She could feel it working – there was just a touch of heat in his eyes. She wondered again if he would make a move – or what she might do if she did.

Instead, he turned to go.

But before he left, he leaned against the door, looking back over his shoulder.

"I saw your text to Maggie Kirkland that night," he said. "I *know*, Kate."

He took a breath.

"We can still stop this."

Kate stared back, giving nothing.

He smiled, nodding to his own blinking message on her phone.

"Call me if you change your mind."

Kate's eyes narrowed. For a guy who wore his heart on his sleeve, he was frustratingly hard to predict.

She hoped he didn't really decide to play hardball. That would be too bad.

Kate was raised on hardball.

"Goodnight, Pete," she said, and closed the door behind him.

Alone in her cheap little room, shivering in her robe and her hair in a towel, Kate took a moment to question herself.

Her mother always taught her to stop and evaluate. When your opposition gives you talking points, you had to address them.

She was well aware of the sensationalism in what she was doing. But she never wavered on higher-morality. The fundraising aspect alone was a windfall for the town, and everyone involved.

Still, she found Pete's accusations bothered her.

She felt judged. And a little bit angry.

And as was her way, *now* she was damned and determined to prove him wrong.

She checked her watch. It was still early, but she still had arrangements and phone calls to make.

Tomorrow was going to be a busy day.

Meanwhile, down in the parking lot, Tommy was waiting in a rented-pick-up, as Pete came down the stairs, grabbing his bag out of the back. Tommy had taken one look at the flea-bitten motel and announced he preferred sleeping on the boat.

"So," Tommy said, "you gonna call the AG?"

Pete shook his head.

"No," he sighed. "She's got my number and she knows it."

"That means you're letting them do it."

Pete didn't know if that was true. Ultimately, he believed he could stir-up whatever hornet's nest he wanted – knowing full-well, if he went to war with Kate Foster on this front, she would not go down alone – and at the end, all these sacrifices would be made and tomorrow would happen anyway.

That was how he would rationalize it to himself, anyway.

"Oh well," Tommy said, shifting the pick-up into gear, "what's the worst that could happen?"

Pete shut his eyes, and just let his imagination run wild.

"Where are you going?" he asked.

Tommy smiled.

"Where do you think? I'm going to get a bigger boat."

CHAPTER 17

Kate puzzled as to why she bothered about Pete Nichols.

They'd been adversaries almost from the moment they met. Not only was he someone who couldn't *do* anything for her – not like dating the governor, or incurring goodwill with a philanthropist billionaire – but he was active opposition right from the start.

Was it just a left-over side-effect? A bonding experience after that night at the rehab facility?

Bruno had sunk the boat ferrying her and Stuart Kirkland to the chopper waiting at the sea wall. Out of all the governor's staff, including Kirkland himself, Kate alone had survived.

She would not deny it was a moment she would never forget when Pete had appeared on the scene, yanking her aboard his own boat like gaffing a trout – and then the race back to the dock, with Bruno hot on their tail, along with Sandy and Ahab, the other two transients.

The orcas had caught them too. But for Corky and the rest of the pod, it would have been all over.

It was strange, Kate thought, in all the old, primitive ways, where it really counted, she and Pete had each other's backs – the sort of trust you never know you can have in a person until you see them tested.

Leave it to the legal system to corrupt all that.

If Pete really did present AG Walker with testimony of Kate's own culpability in Maggie Kirkland's operations, it gave the prosecution evidence of conspiracy. Whether the orcas had escaped because of it – which they hadn't – was irrelevant. A possible independent crime would have been committed.

It would be at the AG's discretion whether to move forward.

Likewise, with Pete's own liability-issue, he could potentially be charged and investigated with negligence resulting in the death of a governor.

It would certainly be scary to be told so by the state.

True, Pete had pulled Kate out of a storming ocean, from the snapping jaws of an angry orca, but that was a different kind of courage.

Pete knew prison-time would be an easy-sell to a Northwest jury, especially after having been widely-branded an expert-for-hire.

Going to the AG could easily hang Pete himself, as much as her.

Kate sincerely hoped Pete didn't.

Should AG Walker come calling, Kate preferred they be on the same side.

Although, her instincts told her, it might actually be better to have a piece of meat to throw Walker's way. Pete *was* made to order.

Inexplicably, Kate found she didn't *want* to.

Perhaps it was because part of her felt *proud* when she'd returned his favor, there at the end, by pulling *him* out of Bruno's jaws, onto the dock – even smacking the big orca with a boat hook, as they scrambled back out of reach.

She had been happy about what that revealed about her character.

To turn around now and throw him under the bus left a bad taste.

For some reason, he made her want to play fair.

That, she thought, was something she needed to get rid of in a hurry. Her mother had taught her that too.

They won't play fair – therefore, neither can *you.*

Kate was bouncing off the walls in the tiny room, with its carpet and linens stinking like mouse-piss. Before today, she hadn't stayed in a dump like this since she was a young child, before her mother had stepped them both up into the big leagues. But you didn't forget mouse-piss.

Pete had been right about one thing. It *was* a come-down.

On impulse, she grabbed up her purse and keys.

There was a little restaurant next door to the motel – The Fish Shack. Perhaps they served drinks.

She kept a wary eye out for Pete, as she crossed the parking lot over to the rustic little diner.

The waitress, whose name-tag identified her as 'Annie', greeted her at the door.

"Get you a booth?" she asked brightly.

But as Kate looked, she realized Cody Martin was sitting by himself at a table near the window overlooking the ocean.

"Actually," Kate said, stepping past Annie, "I think I'll seat myself."

Cody looked up, surprised, as Kate slid in the booth opposite him.

"Well," she said. "Small town."

Cody smiled politely.

"This place is a favorite of mine," he said. "I guess you're at the motel?"

Annie was standing above them, looking uncertain.

"Give you a minute, Cody?" she asked.

"Give us a couple," Kate answered.

Annie's lips pursed slightly, but she stuffed her pen in her hair, and her pad back in her pocket, disappearing into the kitchen.

"Good chowder here," Cody said, neutrally. "Can I help you with something, Ms. Foster?"

"*Kate*," she replied. "Just company."

"I'm not the best company" Cody said. "But if you can take it."

Kate smiled. She could see how Cody could be a bit challenging. She could also see how a lot of young women might respond to it.

He was average-featured, but good-looking in the way of young men, when they were still lithe and muscular. Cody himself was carved from a lifetime on the ocean, and she could see it in the way his shirt hung on his shoulders.

She found herself comparing his youthful physique to her own. She knew perfectly well that, demographically, she was what was known in bars as a 'cougar' – a *little* older, but still hot.

And on the prowl?

Truth to tell, she'd been living celibate since Stuart Kirkland's death, and dating a seventy-year old before that.

She eyed Cody speculatively. She had what? Ten years on him?

Perhaps she was feeling a bit cougar-ish.

Kate nodded to the glass of soda in Cody's hand.

"Not a drinker?" she asked.

Cody tipped his glass. "The district attorney's office thinks it's a good idea." He smiled. "But please, go ahead. Be careful, though. This place makes pretty stiff drinks."

"Well, on *that* note."

Kate smiled, and waved as Annie emerged from the kitchen.

Annie wrote down Kate's order of a rum and coke, stepping over to the bar, and then back a moment later with the drink. She nodded mildly at Cody as she set down the glass.

"Really making the rounds lately," she murmured.

Cody nodded apologetically.

"What's her problem?" Kate asked as Annie retreated back to the kitchen.

"I used to come here a lot with Carson," Cody replied. "She liked Carson."

He nodded to Kate's drink. "And then the last time I was in here, I had to carry Lauren out of here, utterly blotto."

Kate grinned, trying to picture Doctor Palmer stumbling and unable to walk.

"You and Doctor Palmer have an interesting history," she remarked.

"That's a charitable way of putting it," Cody said. "It's the same with all Carson's friends. Carson's whole family. None of them like me much. It's kind of a long story."

"You were involved, and punched out her ex?"

Cody shrugged.

"Alright. I guess it's not that long a story after all."

Kate smiled, sipping at her drink, tasting the alcohol burn. They *did* make them stiff here.

"I suppose," she said, "it's natural for a surfer and a conservationist who wants to protect Great White sharks to be at odds."

Cody's eyes narrowed – clearly that touched a button.

"I think we could have stopped 'conserving' white sharks thirty years ago. I'm of the humble opinion that there isn't a huge ecological need for alpha-predators in a human environment. That's *our* niche."

Kate raised an eyebrow, wondering if he was baiting her. She actually didn't have strong feelings about sharks. On the other hand...

"What about orcas? You think we should hunt them out too?"

Cody held up a finger, as if she had just given up a tell.

"I didn't say hunt them *out*, did I? I said stop protecting them. And it's not the same thing with orcas. They aren't the direct threat to people that sharks are."

He shrugged. "Either way, I don't think nature needs a babysitter. Certainly not someone who thinks they can micromanage it."

He tipped a finger out to the ocean, in evidence.

"As if."

Kate eyed him speculatively.

"You used to fight with Carson quite a lot, didn't you?"

"We might have had our rows," Cody allowed.

Kate found herself smiling, envisioning him at the scene – his roguish good-looks, with its sprinkle of alpha-male arrogance, combined with a handsome, winning smile, that also managed to be just a touch patronizing.

She could see it working on a younger woman.

Of course, Kate was a little older.

Unless she got drunk enough, that is.

She waved at Annie behind the bar.

CHAPTER 18

Early the next morning, Pete was surprised to see Lauren, accompanied by her perky little assistant, Nancy, pulling up into the parking lot of his motel.

Pete and Tommy were already up, waiting on Cody. The motel bordered the fisherman's wharf, catering to recreational fishermen and professional charters, operating up the coast, out of the way of the large commercial docks.

The smallish pier made it all the more apparent that Tommy had followed through on his promise to get a bigger boat.

In point of fact, the vessel had been donated to the Institute by Cousteau's Foundation – a commissioned design, a half-size version of the Mark 1 Class Motor Minesweeper Cousteau used in his films – sixty-feet long, with more technology than the last space-shuttle.

'*The Argonaut*' was painted across the hull.

As she climbed out of her car, Lauren took a long look at the space-aged watercraft docked and waiting.

"That's the *Cousteau* boat," Nancy said, awed.

Pete stepped forward to meet them.

"Doctor Palmer. What are you doing here?"

Lauren was not smiling.

"We are here," she said, "to pick up Kate Foster and take her down to the north docks."

Pete's expression was deliberately neutral.

"My supervisor at the Institute," Lauren continued, "Ms. Cylvia Brown, has informed me that we will be receiving significant funding, and that I am to provide scientific support. On behalf of the Institute."

Lauren took a deep breath.

"And to be of service in any way I can," she finished.

Pete nodded careful understanding.

Lauren eyed him a moment longer, daring *any* comment, before turning to where *The Argonaut* waited at the end of the dock.

"I've been wanting to get on-board that thing since the Institute acquired it. I spent the last two summers working out of off-season charter boats, still smelling of fish-guts, with rusted chains and cages."

She turned accusingly to Pete. "How did *you* get hold of it?"

Tommy waved a hand. "Actually, that was me. I called UW's office and told them I needed a bigger boat. This is what they gave me."

He shrugged apathetically.

"I don't much like it," Tommy complained. "I like something a little smaller, where you can feel the ocean. But it'll have to do, I guess."

Tommy extended his hand to Lauren, introducing himself, and promptly started a fight.

It was actually quite remarkable – it took less than a minute.

"Doctor Palmer," he said, smiling, and pumping Lauren's tentatively-offered hand firmly. "I've heard of you. I was thinking we could help you with your shark problem. All we need to do is call in a bunch of offshore orca pods. They *love* sharks."

Lauren glanced at Pete. "Is he serious?"

Pete shrugged. He was never sure. Personally, he'd heard *worse* ideas.

Tommy was utterly unaffected.

"Why wouldn't I be serious? You've got a population problem. That would solve it."

"By killing them, you mean," Lauren said bitterly.

"Look, Miss," Tommy said, "if your waters are dangerous, addressing it in *any* way is interfering with nature. And when people's lives are at stake, your priority can't be a fish."

Lauren had fallen silent – not conceding the point, in Pete's judgment, so much as counting to ten.

Tommy took the moment to smile winningly at Nancy, who blushed, fluttering.

It had been almost that exact point when Cody's beater pickup turned into the motel parking lot.

Still wearing her clothes from the night before, and looking worse for wear, Kate Foster rode in the passenger seat beside him.

The group of them fell silent, as Cody pulled to a stop.

Pete heard Tommy start to snicker.

Her hair a mess, her sunglasses covering runs in her mascara, Kate rose slowly from Cody's pickup, to regard the entourage waiting in the parking lot.

Confronted by the wall of blinking eyes, Cody simply shrugged.

Kate zeroed in on Lauren's presence first.

"What the hell are *you* doing here?"

Then she leveled her glare at Pete. "What? Is this your new little girlfriend?"

Kate could put a real snarl in her voice, even when she wasn't hungover.

Lauren, struggling to absorb the import of the morning's latest scandal, seemed uncertain how to react.

Pete wasn't quite certain himself.

Pressing her advantage, Kate quickly bore down.

"I'm not kidding, Doctor Palmer. If you're here to impede this operation in any way, I'll have you arrested."

Pete could see Lauren setting her teeth. Beside her, Nancy stood wide-eyed and breathless.

But Lauren held her cool.

"Actually, Ms. Foster," she said, dutifully, "I'm here to *escort* you. The Institute has instructed me to cooperate with you fully."

"Suppose I don't want you?"

"Then call the mayor, and tell him so."

Kate's eyes narrowed. Complete capitulation was what she expected, but was always cautious when it came too easily.

"Alright," she said. "Fine. Give me ten minutes to change."

And with that, Kate turned and stalked past the rest of them, snapping her jacket around her shoulders, pointedly avoiding Pete's eye.

Behind him, Tommy snickered again.

The rest of them turned to Cody, who held up his hands.

"Don't look at me," he said. "Nothing happened."

He nodded to Lauren.

"Seriously," he said. "She doesn't hold her liquor any better than *you* do."

It was a well-placed cheap-shot, especially with Lauren's blood already up.

Cody tilted his head, as if in observation.

"Not resigning in protest, I see."

Lauren glared, and without another word, turned and followed after Kate.

Tagging along beside her, Nancy looked back over her shoulder.

"That's Cody? He's *cute*."

Lauren cast a dire eye sideways, but said nothing.

Cody turned to where Pete and Tommy were gathering their bags. As they headed down to the dock, Tommy socked Cody on the shoulder.

"Dude," he muttered. "*That* was some funny shit."

Pete said nothing, glancing back at the motel, as they loaded their gear on-board.

CHAPTER 19

When Lauren pulled up to the north dock, the beach was already abuzz with tractors and work-crews. There was a single large tug-boat waiting at the end of the pier. The second tug would be working out of the south dock. A helicopter circled above, Lacey Chase, herself, narrating moment-to-moment, the lone network granted air-clearance.

The beach was roped-off as the whales were prepped and readied to be towed, attached by ropes, with crews digging out the wet sand beneath them.

Sightseers gathered along the fenced-off perimeter, but Kate clearly had the support of more than just the city, because Lauren saw state cops working crowd control.

Lauren was impressed and outraged in almost equal measures.

Kate had set this up in two days. It was amazing what money and connections could get done.

Besides the tugs, there was the production's showpiece, the Hawaiian showboat with its underwater windows. This would house the VIP party – celebrities and ticketed guests.

There were, however, also two smaller boats buzzing around between, neither over twenty-five feet – both overloaded with camera equipment and five people deep.

These little out-boards seemed in defiance of Kate's promise of 'bigger boats'.

Lauren wondered if they believed the ecology was like a special effect that could be trusted to wait for its cue.

Kate, apparently having accepted Lauren's indentured presence, made another attempt to bring her on-board.

"Try to imagine seeing this as a Hollywood-level production. The biggest sharks, off the most dangerous beach. The biggest feeding frenzy ever. It's going to be spectacular."

Lauren kept her voice even. She was here on orders, but those orders *were* to provide her expertise.

"It's unethical," she said. "It's also recklessly invasive. You are artificially creating an ecological event for a promotional stunt."

"I think *ecological event* is a bit dramatic." Kate shook her head as if Lauren was somehow not seeing her point. "This *event* will last a few days, tops. It's a non-lethal solution to your shark-problem. The whale carcasses won't stink up the beaches and won't go to waste."

Kate smiled. "And if it just happens to make us a zillion bucks? Well, we're the good guys, right?"

Lauren sighed.

"Excuse me, but doesn't this sound nauseatingly exploitive? Even to you?"

Kate turned on her, one hand on her hip.

"Excuse *me*," she said, "but isn't there an entire film series starring a bunch of sharks and your bare ass?"

Behind her, Nancy chirped.

Lauren blinked. She bit down her immediate reply.

Kate took a long pause, giving Lauren a careful, appraising look.

Lauren found she was caring less by the moment about her job.

In fact, she kind of wanted to *punch* this bitch.

Instead, Lauren remained dutifully silent.

Satisfied, Kate turned to Nancy, thrusting her bag into her hands.

"Here, carry this."

Nancy caught the heavy duffel with a startled '*whoof*'.

"Okay," Kate said, squaring her shoulders and nodding down to the docks. "Let's go to work."

CHAPTER 20

Lauren had to admit, it was something to watch Kate operate.

Just simply walking down to the end of the docks was a gauntlet. Two men, both dressed in nautical gear, probably the tug-captain and his mate, were arguing with a rather wild-eyed fellow holding a clipboard.

"Kate!" wild-eye shouted, waving. "Would you tell this guy who I *am*."

"Captain Blake," Kate said, "this is director, Jerry Renner. Director Renner has produced and directed several successful, award-winning documentaries."

Captain Blake smiled politely. "I appreciate that, ma'am, but Mr. Renner here wants his film-crew's boats too close to my tug."

Jerry turned an earnest eye to Kate.

"You want the quality, you've got to let me operate."

Kate smiled. "That's why we got *you*. Because talent will overcome." But she shook her head. "If Captain Blake says it's a safety issue, then you stay back the required distance. Use zoom."

She turned to the captain and his mate.

"Can you let a cameraman on-board?"

Blake nodded agreeably. "That's not a problem."

Kate nodded to Jerry. "Good enough?"

Jerry scowled. "I'll work with it," he said.

But as Kate started to turn away, Jerry moved into step with her, determined to go over his list.

"We've got our crew set-up on the showboat," he said. "We've got cameras outside and inside. We've got that chopper in the air. We're even attaching cameras under the whales. We're going to have fifty different views we can switch to at any time. And all of it is archival footage for a 'director's cut'."

"And the cast?" Kate asked.

"They're down on the dock, waiting to board. We set-up a little pre-party so they could mingle with the VIP guests," he said. "We sold out on-line in twenty-minutes – thirty tickets."

Now he turned to Lauren and Nancy for the first time. "Who are these two? Actresses?"

"These are my *science* advisers," Kate said. "From the Institute."

Jerry frowned. "Well, then what the hell is *she* doing here?"

Standing there in the middle of the little gathering, waiting to board the showboat – right in among the grouping of semi-famous young nymphs modeling barely-there wear, and polished and tattooed young studs – was Cylvia Brown.

"Oh my God," Nancy said. "I don't believe it."

Lauren repressed a derisive snort. 'Classless and exploitative' was how she'd described *Sharks and Babes,* but today, here was Cylvia, front row.

It must have been a hell of a money deal, Lauren thought.

As Lauren and Nancy walked up with Kate, Cylvia saw them and waved.

"Oh my God," Nancy said, "is she... *smiling*? I don't think I've ever seen that before."

Lauren hadn't either. It actually made her a little nervous.

She almost jumped as another woman's voice spoke behind her, "Excuse me?"

Lauren turned to find herself accosted by a tall, slinky young woman, in sunglasses and a bright red two-piece, with a top that strained against *really* big boobs.

"I'm sorry," the young woman said, smiling brightly, "but aren't you Doctor Lauren Palmer? I've seen your videos. I think they're great."

Lauren smiled politely. She recognized the woman's face, although found herself trying not to stare at the thrusting bosoms practically under her chin.

Up close, they seemed as tight as balloons. Lauren wondered if they would squeak if you rubbed them. The nipples looked as hard as a metal belt buckle.

She forced herself to look in the young woman's eyes.

This must be what it's like to be a *guy*, she thought.

Lauren tried to remember the young actress' name. She'd gotten her break on one of those twenty-somethings party-house reality-shows, and she had been a popular member of the cast. Since then, she'd made several straight-to-cable movies, with guest appearances on as many talk-shows, sit-com, and sporting events as her agent could arrange. More importantly, she had appeared as a host on the last season of '*Shark Week*'.

She had also apparently been cast for the docudrama.

Lauren checked out her boobs again. Could she possibly be playing *her*?

She still couldn't recall her name, but evidently expecting to be recognized, the young woman continued to shake her hand.

"I used to be *so* scared of sharks," she said. "Until I saw your videos. Then I really became fascinated." She smiled proudly. "That's why I did '*Shark Week*'."

Lauren nodded politely, retrieving her hand. But then she felt herself grabbed again as Nancy's fingers dug into her shoulder.

"Oh my God," Nancy whispered, "*Look.*"

The young man separating from the crowd, was the second hot-young cast-member from the party-house, who also happened to have co-hosted 'Shark Week'.

Lauren remembered *his* name – and *not* because he was good-looking, but because he'd marketed himself that way – co-opting the name 'Kenny' – sometimes 'Kenny-Smith', spoken as one word – and parlayed it into a brand.

He was known more for parties than sit-coms. And as Lauren recalled, he had also been an item with the tube-top woman here.

That sparked a memory. At the time, they had picked-up one of those couple-names – *LC/Kenny.*

Liza, Lauren remembered. On the show, they called her Liza. Liza Carter – *LC.*

Kenny was waving, and Liza waved back, even as she turned a slight eye to Lauren.

"I dated him," she said under her breath, through smiling teeth. "He's a total scum-o. Fuck 'em and chuck 'em."

"Liza!" Kenny said brightly, embracing her in a one-armed hug, his other hand holding a mixed-drink. Liza returned the hug and a kiss on the cheek.

Kenny turned to Lauren and Nancy. As he reached out to shake her hand, Nancy looked nearly faint.

"Nice to meet you," Kenny said, giving her his full smile.

"And this," Liza said, as if introducing an old acquaintance, "is Doctor Lauren Palmer."

Kenny turned, extending his hand – his grip was strong, but he held her hand daintily.

"*Doctor,*" he said, "I loved your videos."

Lauren smiled politely. She had heard Kenny's name in her own circles because he was prone to donate money. He had laughed to a reporter how his agent told him it was good PR between benders.

Kenny embraced dramatic-sounding causes. He'd campaigned to introduce grizzly bears into southern Oregon, much to the chagrin of locals. During his *Shark Week* stint, he'd gone cage-diving with Great Whites, and some free-diving with smaller sharks.

He was still holding Lauren's hand. She wondered if he would kiss her knuckles.

It occurred to her that he had probably been cast as Cody.

That almost caused her to snicker.

She was rescued by Liza, who pulled at her other arm, waving as the chopper buzzed close overhead. Lauren could see the intrepid Lacey Chase reporting from the co-pilot's seat.

Both Liza and Kenny held up their drinks in toast, waving to what was now a live-audience.

Lauren looked up at the camera, and so-*much* did not want to be there.

She took in the rest of the cast, and the remarkably beautiful grouping of VIP guests, who were actually difficult to distinguish from the actors. As Kate explained it, most of the tickets for this sort of event were purchased by agents, who dolled them out to clients, providing on-camera exposure.

There was at least one other tall, leggy-blond, practically indistinguishable from Liza Carter. How many women with big boobs did they *need*?

Blondie, Lauren assumed, was to be Carson.

Or, *her* for that matter – people always said she and Carson could be sisters. No reason they couldn't be played by interchangeable bimbos.

There was a little, ferret-faced guy with glasses and a goatee, who Lauren realized was David Templeton's doppelganger.

And of course, there were worker ants between them. The showboat's crew was six-deep, including the captain, but there was also Jerry's film-crew – there was one guy who seemed to be everywhere, running back and forth with lights, cameras, and clipboards. Lauren had no idea what his function was – key-grip, maybe?

There was also an on-floor bartender-slash-waitress, clearly another actress-in-waiting, wearing a bare-midriff cocktail skirt, that revealed a prominent lower-back tattoo – she circled with a tray of drinks deftly balanced on one shoulder.

They all toasted as Lacey Chase's chopper again came in low, circling past the docks, low over the stranded whales, zooming in on the beach-crew's final preparations.

Between both the north and south docks, there was a total of twenty-seven fin whales, likely two pods, twelve beached on the north shore, the rest along with the three sperm whales, further south. Each tug would take their loads on two trips, to a prearranged spot, ten miles past the drop-off, into deep water.

The general plan was, once the sharks were drawn in, to gradually continue towing the carcasses further south and out to sea, leading the sharks with them.

Looking at it optimistically, Lauren acknowledged it likely *would* draw sharks off the coast. Not that there was anything stopping them from turning around and swimming right back after the free meal was gone.

On the other hand, the whole point of the Great Whites' side-trips to the Farallons and Surf Shore each season, was to load up calories for their own oceanic migration.

Might this little venture provide enough pure calories for even this congested population of *big* individuals?

Combined with the presence of orcas in the area, Lauren could see the possibility that the sharks might simply leave.

This entire production was irresponsible, exploitive, and invasive. *And a Hail-Mary.*

But it *might* just work.

Pete's friend Tommy had been right. At this point, any solution was invasion.

Lauren looked down the beach, where the crowds milled behind the fence. Among them were a few protesters. No major groups, not with Kate running things.

But down on the sand was crowded too. Workers with shovels continued to dig under the whales as the tide started to come in, and the tug's engine chugged to life.

The ropes holding the first of the whales grew taut.

A cheer began to rise on the beach, mimicked by those watching from the dock.

Liza and Kenny cheered wildly, arms around each other for the cameras. Blondie and Ferret-face raised their glasses. Even the worker-bee key-grip, and the waitress-with-the-lower-back-tattoo, paused to watch.

Even Nancy was flush with excitement.

Lauren had to admit, her own heart beat a little harder as it all began.

Above it all, Kate watched steadily, the architect overseeing the first ground broken.

It was really going to happen.

How much more, Lauren wondered, could she have done to stop this?

Was she even right for trying?

She had declared her moral high-ground right from the beginning – *imperiously* – to both Cody *and* Doctor Nichols. Yet, here she was.

Not resigning in protest, Cody had said.

The first of the big baleens started to drag. Another cheer rose up from both crowds.

Lacey Chase's chopper hovered overhead as the first half-dozen carcasses slid down the sand into the waiting ocean. Six full-grown fin whales, the largest, nearly eighty-feet long, splashed like giant charging seals into the surf.

The last time Lauren had been out on these waters, she'd seen a single whale cadaver – a *calf* – surrounded by what had to be the largest Great Whites anywhere on the planet.

She'd gotten a good look that day. She had seen what happened when a person fell in among them while they were feeding.

Lauren tried to imagine what it was going to be like out there, just a short while from now.

Ordinarily, Great Whites were very ordered in their habits around a kill. It was a necessity, when you were an alpha-predator, that you minimized fatal inner-species conflict. The biggest sharks ate first – pretty simple – and then they just went in descending order.

On the other hand, when feeding on big whales, Lauren had seen them lined-up like pigs rooting around a trough.

But with *this* much stimulus? Great White sharks didn't usually have true feeding frenzies like some of the *carcharhinid* shark species, but that was at least partially because there was rarely that much meat on hand to warrant that sort of out-of-control, piranha-like aggression from a two-ton predator.

Not this time.

And it wasn't just *big* sharks out there – it was a LOT of big sharks.

Lauren could already imagine the water beginning to boil.

Although, she reassured herself, this time she really *was* getting a bigger boat. That was at least one note of confidence. Design-wise, the showboat was basically a small ferry, that was not getting sunk by *any* shark.

On the other hand, there were still those key-grippers buzzing around in their outboards.

Under normal circumstances, they probably would be safe – not like Carson's rickety fourteen-footer.

Unfortunately, there was nothing normal happening today.

Lauren still remembered the shock in her feet as Rhonda had hit their charter boat – and the moment she realized it had been enough to sink them.

And then, sliding into the water, in among all those circling fins.

What would it be like out there today?

Lauren looked out at the deceptively empty ocean and shivered.

CHAPTER 21

The tugs started at opposite ends of the five-mile stretch of beach. Captain Blake's boat, working out of the north dock, pulled its load first.

More cheering echoed down the beach as the massive shapes stretched out behind the boat in tandem, each pulling up a wake like a small submarine. The tug engines worked at a good easy pace, unstrained – boats intended to pull ships.

The second load came from the south beach, including the three cachalots.

Doby was drifting below the surface, hovering near the bottom in the shallows, right before the drop-off, just as he had for the past three days.

At times, he had been sleeping. He rose once upon the hour to spout.

He was still suffering from his wounds, but nevertheless continued to loiter in what he knew were increasingly unstable waters.

The ocean *sounded* dead today.

There were no cries of baleens. Along this migration, nearly an entire wave of this year's pods had either beached or been taken. Besides the two groups along Surf Shore, at least three other pods had beached further along the coast.

Doby could also still hear the lost cries of the orphaned cachalot adolescents.

They sounded hungry, stumbling their way around their hunting. They were still skittish, but the fact that they hadn't completely fled the region, meant their stomachs were talking. The underwater canyons were a deep-ocean food-stop for cachalots, and for all they knew, the rogue orca pod might follow them right along the migratory highway and run them down, anyway.

So, might as well eat.

Doby could respect that.

He had called out to them again, and this time, the largest of the three had approached.

Doby had hovered – not threatening, although clearly letting the youngster see his size – but also indicating he might be willing to tolerate their presence.

Still lacking nerve, the trio had done a quick fade.

Doby understood. Their own scars were too fresh – especially in view of his own open wounds.

Retreat was likely the better part of valor, anyway. Things had gotten worse.

Humans were arriving in numbers. That was never good.

Yet Doby still clung doggedly to the coast, never more than a mile from the beach where the remains of Berta's pod lay.

One can wonder at the limits of Doby's understanding, or why he might continue to linger, both in the combined presence of humans *and* orcas.

As he hung suspended down below, seventy-feet and sixty-five tons of angry, wounded muscle, one might also wonder how he might feel about seeing his mate and offspring towed away like so much garbage?

Like so much *carrion*?

One can only speculate.

Outwardly, there was his scarred and expressionless face, staring up, as the tug from the south beach crossed the surface. Berta and the calf were tethered to the outside, the dead infant bouncing against the larger female's dead hide against the pull of the water.

For long moments, Doby hung motionless.

Then his massive, seemingly ponderous weight shifted in the water, light as a bird on a wing.

The tug passed above, headed out to sea.

Doby turned to follow.

CHAPTER 22

The most basic instincts always decided things, Pete thought.

He had to respect Cody. Obviously recognizing the potential sore spot, the young man had taken the direct approach, making a point to reemphasize that nothing happened with Kate last night.

"Seriously," he said, "she got hammered on oyster-shooters and puked cocktail-sauce and vodka."

Tommy snickered.

"*And,*" Cody added, "she's a belligerent drunk."

Pete, who had never seen it, was willing to believe it.

Still, he was a *guy*, so he said, "What makes you think I care?"

Cody had simply given him a look. *Dude, please.*

Pete chuckled. The lack of pretense was refreshing.

"Okay," he said. "I care just enough to be irritated."

"Personally," Cody said, "I'd run."

"And she's a *bitch!*" Tommy volunteered.

"Okay, okay," Pete said, waving his hand.

Tommy eyed Cody.

"If she was that drunk, why didn't you take her back to the motel? How'd you end up at your place?"

Cody shrugged.

"Well, I didn't *know* she was that drunk at first."

Tommy nodded. "That's better."

Cody turned apologetically to Pete.

Pete waved it off. "Forget about it. Not an issue."

As far as Kate went, there was never going to be an easy day.

He wondered what was going on back at the beach. Today, they were semi-purposely several miles south.

Pete had gotten a text from Kate, informing him that there would be no unauthorized personnel, boats, or vehicles allowed within the operation's ten-mile perimeter, or a thousand yards of the tug routes.

Apparently, just in case he had a mind to be.

Kate had a way to her. They were already headed the other direction, but now he found himself chaffing that it *looked* like he was being ordered off.

He was sure Kate knew she was subtly pushing his buttons.

Nevertheless, the day's trip really had been pre-planned. Cody had again directed them around the south-point, but this time, instead of hovering around the coast, they'd headed for deep water.

It was always a little intimidating once you got more than a few miles out into open ocean, after the crest of land had truly fallen away.

At least today, Pete thought, they were going in style.

The Argonaut. A gift from the Cousteau Foundation. Not too shabby.

He grinned a little. Lauren had been absolutely *green*.

Tommy chopped through the heavy swells with barely a bump.

They were headed a lot further out today. The transients weren't answering their calls, although Tommy said he was certain they were still prowling about. Today, they were looking for the off-shore pods.

Once they got a few miles out, Tommy started playing the stereo, the second-half of Pink Floyd's *The Wall*.

"We'll see if Calypso's around," he said.

"That," Cody remarked quietly, "was Lauren's nickname for Carson. Spirit of the sea."

Tommy nodded. "Calypso's a tough old matriarch that's usually leading her team down the coast this time of year. She should be in the area."

"They'd be hard to miss," Pete agreed. "The offshore types go in big pods. Two hundred members, sometimes. Calypso's is the largest pod on the coast."

"And she likes Floyd?" Cody asked.

"I think preferences distinct to eco-types have to do with how they resonate with their specific languages," Pete volunteered. "What most resembles the sounds they make themselves."

Tommy nodded. "Probably not far off."

He stopped the music, switching tracks.

"Here, listen."

Now he played recordings of orca pods, switching from one track to the other. Each had a distinct and different sound.

"Those ones that sound like they're on helium," Tommy said, "those are the Antarctic types. Completely different from what you get up north in British Columbia, where they have these long, drawn-out calls. Then down in New Zealand, they have an Australian twang."

"So basically, you've learned to imitate the sound of different pods with your flute," Cody said.

"That's the superficial part of it. But the common thread among all the dialects is that the message is in the inflection."

"Sounds more like the sort of thing you do with a sax. Like jazz."

Tommy nodded again. "That's not far off."

He considered. "Maybe I should learn saxophone."

"I'm sure you could get the university to pay for lessons," Pete said dryly.

"Probably," Tommy agreed, making a mental note.

Pete looked back towards shore, miles out of sight. So far, the ocean was still empty.

"Think we're out far enough?"

Tommy glanced back, and cut back on the engine, handling the hefty cruiser like a ski boat, riding the swells without a ripple, as he coasted to a stop.

So far, the music was attracting little attention. Tommy switched over to recordings of the off-shore pods, and their own unique, busy, chirping variation of the orca song.

Still nothing.

"I *know* Calypso's pod is down here this time of year," Tommy said. "I suppose they could be a ways further out. They tend to hang pretty far off shore when they're up north.

"And," he added, "that's also where they're used to seeing me. Maybe I'm breaking etiquette."

But Tommy frowned. Pete could see it was bothering him. He wasn't used to being snubbed.

"You think this is because of your orcas?" Tommy asked.

Pete nodded slowly. Yes, he did.

"Maybe," Tommy said, turning the boat back towards shore, "it's time we start focusing on finding *them*."

Pete shook his head. "They *know* we're looking for them."

"Then that means they're probably listening," Tommy said. "Maybe we can talk them into it."

Once the shoreline came back into view, he tapped the stereo back on – more whale songs.

"These are the tapes you sent me from the facility," he said. "If they're about, it should get their attention."

Tommy stopped the boat.

Around them, the ocean was as empty as ever.

They sat there, looking around the seemingly dead sea, listening to the varied drawls of clicks and squeaks echoing over the speakers.

Nothing.

Finally, Pete reached over and shut off the stereo, grabbed up the microphone and hollered into the speaker.

"Hey Corky! You out there? Any of you guys? It's Pete!"

A pause of silence.

"Goddamnit, where the hell are you?"

And suddenly the water beside the boat erupted.

The Argonaut's top rail was nearly twelve feet above the water, yet the ocean rose up in a flood, drenching the three men in icy brine.

In the middle of the deluge, coming completely clear of the water, turning in a spiraling corkscrew, was the mottled harlequin shape of Corky – sending a wave over the railing as she had done a thousand times for tourists – as she had done many times to Pete himself.

Corky paused in mid-air – orca hang-time – seeming to grin cheekily before crashing back down, drenching them all once again.

Pete nodded to the others, wiping saltwater from his eyes.

"It's her favorite trick," he said. "Trust me. It never gets old."

As Corky breached again, she was now joined by the others.

Big brother Orky, jealous of the attention, leaped up even higher than his sister. And then suddenly the ocean came alive with giant black-and-white shapes, and the boat was surrounded by tall black fins.

The old Skipper, his fin drooping, swam in close.

Pete stood looking down over the railing as the aging male turned in the water.

What was he seeing? Pete wondered. Was the old orca reveling in his freedom, perhaps for the first time in his life?

Or, perhaps was the Skipper seeing Pete, and longing to be back home where it was safe?

All the time he'd spent with orcas, and he still couldn't read their most basic moods.

He suspected it wasn't that way for them, when it came to reading *him*.

"They're happy to see you," Tommy said, squeezing water out of his shirt. "Especially that big female."

Cody hung back respectfully away from the railing. Corky's initial jump had been above their heads.

In the water below, each of the escapees seemed to be making a pass, showing off, as orcas were prone to do. Merry and Pippin, both residents like Orky and Corky, also breached, followed by the tail-walking Marty Feldman.

A bit more reluctant were Ahab and Sandy – both transients. Last time they'd met, they had helped Bruno sink his boat.

Pete remained pretty sure they hadn't actually killed anybody.

"Hey guys," he said, as they passed.

As if to acknowledge, Sandy flapped her fluke.

Now Corky came in again, rolling in the water.

Pete could see her belly – not overt yet, but she was looking round.

Pregnant alright.

Pete glanced where Ahab hung back at a distance, watching carefully. Pete eyed him right back. Attacks on trainers had occurred in parks by the males of mated pairs, who became territorial and aggressive.

Corky seemed to sense his apprehension, and flapped her tail for attention.

Pete smiled down.

"It's good to see you, too," he said.

Pete glanced at Tommy.

Well, he thought, what now?

The creature before him was just that – an animal – and as much empathy as he might feel for her, Corky was, in her way, as alien to his understanding as a being from space.

He couldn't even talk to her – not even to say something as simple as *'stop killing so damned many whales'* – a basic communication that would solve everything, that was also impossible.

How was it that this creature was his friend?

And as Corky rose up out of the water, spy-hopping just out of reach of his out-stretched hand, Pete found himself nearly tearing-up.

It just *was*.

He loved her. He wanted so much to help and he didn't know how.

And he *so much* didn't want to see her get hurt.

Behind him, he heard an electronic beep.

It was Cody's phone – the ringtone was the theme from JAWS.

"Sorry," Cody said, pulling his phone out of his pocket, "they gave me a free-order to the live-feed." He tapped his screen alive.

His face slowly folded into a frown.

"Uh, guys," he said, looking down at the screen, "I think we've got a problem."

Tommy and Pete exchanged glances as Cody held the image up for them to see.

It took a moment for the full import to fully register.

Pete had been afraid of a perfect storm.

Once again, he had low-balled. Badly.

"We've got to get there," Pete said. *"Now."*

CHAPTER 23

Lieutenant Hendricks waved to the tug captain as the big boat rumbled by.

On a normal day, a tug that size would crew maybe six. Today, Hendricks saw at least ten.

The Coast Guard was there today to provide escort for the operation. The only problems so far were a few protesters who had gathered in boats, obviously intending to block passage.

Kate Foster had been on top of that, specifically warning Hendricks' office to be prepared for just that sort of thing.

There actually weren't all that many of them, and Hendricks was relieved. He had seen protests in large numbers create wildly dangerous situations, and as a rescue worker, that was something that tried his patience.

The scattered boats out there today were not part of any big-money group. These guys looked fairly low-rent.

Hendricks wasn't even sure what their specific beef was. The whales were dead.

Desecration of an endangered corpse?

He'd gotten some rather incoherent, but clearly outraged anecdotes from one boat-full that had pressed close enough to the barrier that Hendricks was forced to chase them back.

It was a patch-work boat, captained by an elderly professorial fellow, white-bearded, and accompanied by a much-younger, remarkably attractive, all female crew. White-beard had a loudspeaker, and broadcasted a variety of concerns, from the invasion of the ocean, exploitation of resources, to conservation of whales *and* sharks, and instructed Hendricks to GOOGLE it, if he didn't believe him.

White-beard had pointed an accusatory finger as Hendricks pulled up beside their little boat, "If you're not part of the solution, you're part of the problem."

His college-age harem catcalled affirmatively.

Hendricks smiled politely.

"You've given me a lot to think about," he said. "Just please keep back behind the buoys."

Lieutenant Hendricks was acting head of the local Guard office in Quinton Shaw's absence, and he was quickly discovering he didn't like being in charge. Near as he could tell, it mostly meant taking phone calls he didn't want, all day long.

He much preferred getting out and performing the rescue.

Picking up that particular slack also left him all the more aware Quinton was gone. And a *bad* death.

But Hendricks was a professional. He was polite to the activists that told him he was helping to destroy the ecology, reminding himself they didn't know, only a few days ago, that same ecology had taken the life of a good friend.

The swell of the tug's passing lifted Hendricks' own boat with its greater weight, followed by the passage of its load of dead whales.

There were generalized heckles and boos from the gathering of boats.

To a certain extent, Hendricks understood.

It was a sad and ugly image, all that death. He hated to see it.

One of the smaller whales, the sperm whale calf, was propped up so that its torn and distended lower jaw jutted up into the air.

Hendricks frowned. What the hell could have done that? Surely not a shark?

As the tug began to pull away, he took out his binoculars.

A helicopter circled in the distance, marking the rendezvous spot from the air.

Just below, the showboat was traveling in tandem with the first tug.

Hendricks almost had to laugh. Lauren, of all people, had managed to find herself on-board. She had actually called him just last night, asking if there was anything he could do to put a block on this whole operation.

Hendricks had apologized.

"I'm afraid you're over-estimating my influence. I'm just a paramedic on the water."

"Yeah," she said, uncharacteristically sour, "I've been hearing that a lot, just lately."

He had promised to make a few calls, feeling ridiculously bureaucratical as he did so. Was that his job now? Bullshitting people who apparently believed he had influence on policy?

Now that he thought about it, Quinton had often rolled a cynical eye when he affectionately mentioned the 'dear-public'. Hendricks belatedly recognized how deftly Shaw had taken-on that part of the job.

But Hendricks would not let it be said that he had willfully put anyone in the public at risk. Lauren wasn't just the kid he and Quinton had pulled out of one ornery prank after another – she was a doctor in her field and she had come to him as an expert.

When he had dutifully told his superiors at the state office about *Doctor* Lauren Palmer's list of concerns, Hendricks was informed that he himself was going to be there, on the spot, *and* directing traffic.

And just because Lauren was Lauren, had she or had she not found herself right in the middle of it? Right on-board the same damned showboat, she'd been determined never leave shore.

Ya had to love her. Lauren was likely a cat on the ceiling.

Still, in the larger scheme, Hendricks didn't really see the problem.

Something had to be done with whales, and if it saved the city the expense, that was something to tell the tax-payers.

From the production Hendricks saw being put together, the broke and starving town actually stood to make a *lot* of money – something that was not a bad thing for a change.

He also liked the idea of returning the sheer biomass back to the sea. He was no environmentalist, but anyone that pursued a life on the ocean had an appreciation for nature and the whole cycle-of-life bit. He hated waste.

Lauren was a good kid, and smart as a whip, but she was a typical idealist. And to tell the truth and shame the Devil, too many people thinking like she did, goodhearted or not, had gone a long way towards *creating* the problems that existed at Surf Shore.

She had loved Quinton, and Hendricks wouldn't ever say it to her, but he saw a wisp of responsibility for Shaw's death on Lauren's own shoulders, just by virtue of advocacy.

He might remind her, going forward, that meant *her* opinions as a scientist had influence on the policy *he* was supposed to act upon.

Hendricks sighed, looking out after the big tug.

Today, at least, he foresaw nothing more than a simple clean-up operation – larger-scale, with more publicity than most, and unusual in the amount of bio-mass, but no more than daily-chores for the tug operators.

Beyond the obvious heightened risk of simply falling in, of course.

The swells from the tug and its cargo had passed, but suddenly Hendricks felt another lift in the water, as if something large had passed by.

He turned, frowning, as he scanned the smattering of protest-boats, none big enough or close enough to create that sort of swell.

After a moment, he picked up his phone, tapping up the screen.

"This is Hendricks," he said. "The first load from the south beach is through. Should be heading your way."

Kate Foster's voice spoke in his ear.

"Thanks, Len. Any trouble?"

"Nah. Just a few boats. A few signs with slogans. Everyone's mostly behaving."

"Good to hear it. Keep me posted."

Kate blinked off, and Hendricks turned to watch the departing tug.

The mysterious swell wasn't repeated.

He wondered what it was like at the site. By now, the first load from the north beach should be dropped, sending the tug back for seconds.

Hendricks tapped his phone again and an image from the showboat appeared – he'd been provided a live-feed.

One thing about these Hollywood-types, they put cameras everywhere. He was confident anything that happened, they would be well on top of it.

And, he thought, somewhat ruefully, it would be well-documented.

Right now, the image was from the chopper, with staccato commentary from Lacey Chase – dark-haired, dark-eyed, and good-looking enough to do cutaways, even when she was strapped in chopper-goggles and a headset.

The chopper was circling the showboat, while the tug-workers released and secured its first load.

The view switched between multiple angles, from the tug, to the showboat itself. There were even cameras attached underneath the floating whales, blinking different images of rolling carcasses and the deep blue gloom beneath.

Hendricks wondered if the sharks were picking up on any of it yet.

The cameras so-far revealed nothing but empty gloom.

Out on the surface, there was also a lot of big blue nothing.

Of course, they hadn't seen anything when Quinton had been taken either.

The sharks were there alright.

It was only a matter of time and those underwater cameras were going to start picking up something interesting.

CHAPTER 24

The Ultimate Great White Feeding Frenzy – its official last-minute title – went live at ten a.m. western.

Kate had wanted to wait until they made sure the first sharks had appeared on the scene.

As it turned out, that wasn't going to be a problem.

Between the live-feed, the tow-operation, coordinating the actors and VIP guests, along with the producers, that was the one thing that was going to happen without supervision.

Lauren tried to imagine Cylvia Brown trying to handle all those moving parts.

Stern, dour Cylvia, currently mingling with the pretty people.

Nancy had shaken her head as she watched. "You think she's drunk?"

Liza of the tube-top and big-boobs had twice moved-in to intercept Kenny's cheerful, sweeping passes by both Lauren and Nancy. He'd also done a quick fly-by over Blondie, much to the obvious chagrin of ferret-face.

Kate had nodded at the waitress-with-the-lower-back-tattoo to scale-down Kenny's high-octanes.

Liza had apologized to Lauren.

"That's how Hollywood is," she said. "It's an easier *in* if you're a pretty woman, but you're a dime-a-dozen. The big good-looking studs are rarer. They get treated like the king lion. It doesn't take them long to figure it out."

Kenny had taken that moment to circle in again. Liza nodded at Lauren knowingly, as she allowed his hand to encircle her waist, and diverted him deliberately away.

Director Jerry was growing impatient.

"I think we should start chumming."

Kate had deferred to Lauren.

"You're towing several hundred tons of free meat," Lauren said. "I think chum is a little redundant, at this point."

She turned, peering out the window – solid, transparent poly-carbonate, guaranteed not to break.

Yes, Lauren *had* asked.

The view-windows looked up underneath the floating carcasses, which were crowded together like logs.

Below, the endless blue remained seemingly empty.

Lauren shook her head, knowing better than to believe it.

"Trust me," she said. "They're already here."

She nodded affirmatively to Kate, and then to Jerry.

"When things settle down for a minute, they'll show themselves."

She pointed to the news-chopper hovering above.

"You might have them hold back until things get started."

Kate nodded, tapping her phone and bringing up Lacey Chase.

"Pull back," she said, "half a mile, until I say so."

"But, *wait...*" Lacey Chase blurted before Kate clicked her off.

After a moment, seemingly disgruntled, the hovering chopper pulled back to hover at almost exactly half-a-mile, like a dog at the very end of its leash.

Jerry Renner was likewise pawing at the ground.

"Anybody out there at all?" he barked, simultaneously into his headset and into the face of the nervous-looking key-grip. "Anybody sees even a fin, you let me know."

He glared at Kate. "We go live within the hour," he said.

Lauren eyed Jerry uncomfortably. Being in too big a hurry made you reckless.

After the second tug brought the first load from the south beach, she had actually seen the tug-crew walking on top of the tethered whales as they floated.

Lauren wondered how slippery that wet, decomposing blubber might be.

She had once seen an on-video stunt, where a cameraman had crawled out onto the floating carcass of a dead whale, surrounded by feeding white sharks.

The footage was undeniably dramatic – he'd placed his camera not a foot away from massive jaws, tearing out two-foot chunks of whale. In the background, you could hear his worried fellows exhorting him to come back in. At the time, Lauren couldn't have imagined anything so utterly foolish.

Today, she saw men hopping from whale to whale like they were tethering up a garbage barge.

Carson had been widely-criticized for her free-swim with Bloody Mary. But even that was not as cavalier as it appeared. It was like approaching lions or bears, or any large predator. It was all about gauging their moods. Carson was very good at that.

But free-swimming with a twenty-foot white, that you'd scouted-out for a half-hour, was one thing. It was never the shark you *could* see that was the problem.

It was when they hovered below, just out of sight, draped in that cloak of invisibility, where their natural coloring merged perfectly with the gloom.

When they were *looking* for you.

Jerry's speaker beeped. A female voice chirped in excitement.

"I got something, boss!"

"Go!" Jerry barked into his head-set.

The showboat's big screens suddenly blinked to an image from beneath one of the whales.

Rising up slowly, as if out of mist, was the first inquisitive shadow of a shark.

It was somewhere out there now, Lauren thought, just outside the hull of this very boat. So far, their double-load of carcasses counted fifteen-deep, stretched within the length of a football field, but that still was past the point of visibility underwater.

Something she always found fascinating about white sharks – which actually felt a little bit eerie, right about now – was how you never *saw* any of them, but then suddenly there were half-a-dozen, all at once.

That was when you realized they had been there all along.

She used to chide surfers for fear of sharks, because they were *always* there, often within yards of you, checking you out – and it was mostly to make sure they didn't *want* you.

Unfortunately, that was an equation based on stability.

Such was not the case off Surf Shore.

The shark that rose majestically from below was a big, powerfully-built female, easily eighteen-feet long, and she was now being broadcast worldwide. As her image flashed on the showboat's view-screens, there was a whoop of excitement

It was not an animal Lauren recognized, which was significant in and of itself, considering she and Carson had been cataloging sharks in these waters for years. An animal of this size going completely unnoticed seemed unlikely. It was no Big Rhonda, but still certainly a monster Great White.

That sneaky little seal colony had changed things.

Until five or six years ago, this animal might have continued along her normal migration, way out to sea, perhaps swerving in near the Farallons, but there would have been no reason for a big, energy-conserving creature like this to venture into these waters.

When push came to shove, it was always about how much biomass was there to support the ecology.

Animals went where the food was.

The big shark rose slowly, nuzzling at the first of the dead whales, floating as if drifting on the scent.

And then, just like that, there were three more of them – another big female and two large males.

Lauren recognized Jabberjaw. The other male was new, but at least seventeen feet – damn near as big as males got.

And yet another eighteen-plus-foot female.

Jerry's speaker beeped. The woman's voice again.

"We're getting them all over, sir,"

"Everyone with a hit, go live, all at once," he said. "Every screen."

Now the widescreens on the showboat split into at least-two-dozen views.

Then Liza cried out, standing at the view-port, pointing outside.

"Oh my God, look at that!"

Just outside the portal, Lauren recognized Mack the Knife, one of the most aggressive males in the region, and Lauren's pick as the number-one candidate for the mating scars all over the region's big females, like Rhonda and Bloody Mary.

Mack rose with boldness, latching onto the closest whale – the sperm whale calf.

Within moments, three other males appeared, all of them converging aggressively on the floating carcass.

More sharks were circling below, and far from the ordered procession Lauren had always observed with Great Whites, these sharks were posturing, back arched, fins poised and spread.

Lauren felt a touch of disquiet.

Beyond the sheer bio-mass necessary to stimulate it, there was a practical reason white sharks didn't engage in the out-of-control feeding frenzies common among other deep ocean species, like blue sharks, tigers, white-tips and black-tips – they were too damned powerful.

The big Carcharodons were meant to be, by and large, solitary hunters, and certainly never in the congested numbers as they were in this spot, here today.

Already they were turning on each other.

Mack snapped aggressively at his not-much-smaller mate, who, in turn, snapped at the third.

The screens showed the same thing everywhere. The above-surface cameras caught the thrashing of massive, five-foot tails, as the tethered whales were tugged and rocked from below.

One of the underwater cameras had already been hit. The view-screen showed a massive, jagged maw clamping down, and then went blank. Another cheer went up on the showboat, this time accompanied by a round of applause.

"Copy that," Jerry said immediately. "Put it out on the web with a link."

Lauren looked in wonder at the multiple screens, each a mirror of the scene playing out just on the other side of the window.

She had never seen so many large sharks in her life. Not even on the charter boat.

Liza suddenly cried out again.

The tugging, mauling sharks, brawling over the baby cachalot, suddenly broke to either side, including the belligerent Mack the Knife.

Out of nowhere, a massive shark launched up from below.

Twenty solid feet, two-and-a-half tons, blasting up at thirty miles-an-hour, an enormous female hit the sperm whale calf, knocking it squarely out of the water, tearing it loose from its moorings – carving her own carcass off from the others, as if planned.

Lauren recognized the massive, scarred juggernaut as the big female crashed back down, a massive bite of *her* whale bulging from her jaws.

"Hello, Mary," Lauren said quietly.

Beside her, Kate motioned to Jerry, pointing out the window as the massive fish paraded past.

"There's our star," Jerry said, nodding.

The main screen switched to Bloody Mary as her jaws latched onto the whale once again, pushing the smaller calf away from the others.

Lauren leaned close to the glass as the big shark tore away a mouthful, her throat bulging like a python as she gulped down the two-hundred pound chunk of blubber.

Was it you, Mary? Lauren wondered.

Mary had been a suspect for the Surf Shore killer all along. It was just that Rhonda had always seemed a lot *better* suspect.

But Rhonda was gone.

And besides Quinton, yet another surfer had been taken.

Mary was always the sneaky one. The one that came up from behind.

Although, certainly, she was acting out today in much bolder fashion than Lauren had ever seen before.

Rhonda had been the bully. Perhaps Mary was filling that niche too.

Now that Mary had pushed the calf sufficient distance, Mack and some of the others were cozening back up, simply moving on to the next carcass over.

Lauren heard a beep beside her, and Kate glanced at her phone.

She smiled sideways at Lauren.

"My producers," she said. "Pay-per-view orders are doing *very* well."

Now Jerry was grinning as he switched the main feed from screen to screen, editing on the fly, like a DJ spinning an album.

Lauren couldn't even estimate how many sharks. From her vantage, each whale was being mobbed by at least half-a-dozen, while others circled below, none less than fifteen-feet long, in her view – very large, adult members of both sexes.

Fun fact: white sharks were known to bite each other completely in half when they got *too* excited.

From the showboat's cameras, it looked like the two smaller boats were edging in among them.

"That's not safe," Lauren said, quickly.

Kate glanced at her. "What?"

"Those outboards are getting too close."

Kate nodded to Jerry. "Get them back."

Looking chagrined, Jerry dutifully carried out the order.

Lauren turned away, almost frustrated at the prompt correction. So far, Kate seemed to be on top of every concern.

Without something specific she could cling to, all Lauren had was a mounting feeling of dread. And that wasn't scientific advice. That was, *I'm scared and I want to go home.*

No less true.

Cody had said it best. There was something *wrong* with this place.

And while the two outboards dutifully pulled back, Lauren could clearly see the sharks themselves were now showing interest – getting a little wild, in fact, rocking them, smacking their hulls with flapping tails.

Some of the on-board comments made it through the live-feed – a few startled profanities, along with some nervous laughter.

Similar nervous laughter echoed through the showboat. The small audience was rapt.

Kate's phone beeped again.

"More pay-per-view numbers, I'm sure," she said, smiling as she reached into her pocket.

The smile broke, however, when she saw the caller ID.

Lauren caught the sudden frown.

Kate tapped the screen and Lieutenant Hendricks popped up.

When Lauren saw his ashen face, she was reminded of the night he told her Quinton Shaw had been killed.

"Kate," Hendricks said. "We've got trouble."

And as he spoke, for the first time in the years since she'd known him, Lauren heard fear in his voice.

"A boat's gone down," he said.

CHAPTER 25

The second tug was halfway back to the south beach when it was hit.

Lieutenant Hendricks had dutifully logged its passing, again waving to the captain as he went by – a crusty old codger named Mills, who had been a guardsman, years ago, now retired, living on a comfortable pension, supplemented by applying his skills as a tug-boat operator.

Hendricks had never done the math, but expected Mills to be well-compensated for life, and had once asked why the old-man stayed on the water.

"Where else would I be?" Mills had replied. "I'm getting paid to drive a boat."

Fair enough, Hendricks thought. Not exactly a bad way to end up himself.

His phone beeped, and he looked down to the message that the first tug had arrived with their second load.

According to his live-stream, the north beach was now clear, although the police hadn't opened it back up to the public – not until the second tug cleared its last load.

Lacey Chase was doing another brief on-camera. Hendricks had a thing for Lacey Chase, ever since she'd interviewed him last year, after a boat-wreck that had been bad enough to make the news.

He remembered trying to sound terribly official, but she had nevertheless caught that twinkle in his eye, and had just given him the *best* smile.

When she came on, he gave her a moment's attention.

Thus, he missed the initial impact when the tug was struck from below.

There was a heavy boom, and when Hendricks looked up, the big tug was suddenly askew in the water.

The impact was followed by a sudden echoing ruckus from the scattered boats of protesters, accompanied by clicks of radios and blinking phones. The junker-boat was again cresting the buoys.

Scratchy with static, the white-beard's voice carried electronically, broadcast over his mega-phone, "What the hell was that?"

There was answering static, as Hendricks' own radio barked alive.

Mills, who he had just been waving to, was shouting over the air.

"Jesus! Something *hit* us! We're taking on water!"

Hendricks blinked, and nearly missed the impact a second time.

114

The entire frame of the tugboat shook, as if striking an unforgiving reef.

And just like a reef, it gouged the bottom of the boat like a can-opener.

In the space of seconds, the sixty-five-foot vessel listed, tilting like a rubber-duck in a bathtub. Hendricks could see the overloaded crew scrambling on deck, some already leaping over the side.

Hendricks looked around helplessly at his own thirty-footer. He couldn't fit a dozen men on-board. He grabbed his radio to call for help.

The tug was hit again. And this time he *saw* it.

A huge squared head, followed by a massive, smashing tail.

Hendricks couldn't believe it. A whale.

He heard screams from the young crew on white-beard's boat.

Their motor fired up, and Hendricks saw them steer past the buoys, apparently intending to lend the tug-crew a hand.

For a moment, he was tempted to let them, but their little junker shouldn't be out this far, anyway. As he leaned on this own throttle, motoring towards the flailing tug, he turned on his own loudspeaker.

"Civilians, please," he barked. "Stay back behind the boundaries. Emergency rescue is on its way."

Hendricks could see white-beard holding up his middle finger as he leaned on his own throttle.

This time, the cachalot rose up from below.

Hendricks gasped at the size of its body as the whale breached.

The full length – seventy-feet or better by Hendricks' eye – came up through the middle of white-beard's little junker.

Hendricks saw their bodies go flying as the boat was blasted into the air and demolished.

There were small, unimportant-sounding splashes as they hit the water.

In the swelling surf, Hendricks was only able to spot two of the young women, who both floated limply.

The big whale, however, was not done. A montage of screams erupted as the swell of ocean arrowed directly into the scattered protesters – not targeting any individual, just plowing right through the middle.

Three boats were swamped. A fourth took a direct blow and was broken apart.

Hendricks was momentarily torn, but erring on the side of the civilians, he turned his boat in the direction of the first two floating bodies.

But then, the big whale turned in *his* direction.

Hendricks paused on the throttle, facing the beast as it spouted – a dragon's snort – like a bull pawing the dirt before a charge.

For a split second, Hendricks' hand hovered over the throttle, ready to crank hard starboard, should the beast attack.

If he could get a little room, he had a rifle secured on-board.

But then the whale sounded, dropping below the surface.

Hendricks could see the massive shape passing below.

It was headed out to sea, following unerringly along the demolished tug-boat's path.

Hendricks could see Lacey Chase's news-chopper circling in the distance, marking the site from above.

Even as he flashed the emergency signal on his radio, Hendricks' other hand reached for his phone, calling Kate Foster.

CHAPTER 26

Bloody Mary cruised between the showboat and the cachalot calf.

By either accident or design, she had nudged the floating carcass almost right next to the showboat. She could see the humans peering out the windows.

In Mary's world, humans were a fairly nasty form of prey – and frustratingly abundant in areas where a passing Great White might reasonably expect to be sinking her teeth into a nice plump mouthful of elephant seal. By Mary's standards, sort of a junk-fish.

She also knew they could be dangerous, and were best avoided in large numbers.

In what looked like deliberate display, Mary passed close to the showboat, prompting excited reaction on the other side of the glass.

Behind her, the other sharks tore away at the rest of the banquet. None had yet dared intrude on Mary's private buffet.

That was probably wise. Mary's blood was up. What with Rhonda not there to enforce discipline among the subjects, and the near-intoxication of so much food in the water, Bloody Mary was quite ready to chomp anyone or anything in range, right in half, at the drop of a dime.

The baby cachalot shook as she tore out an enormous bite.

There were flashes of light from the boat, as the humans held up their little devices.

Then, abruptly, Mary pulled away from the baby whale.

Her senses were picking up something moving in from below – something BIG.

The other sharks sensed it as well, and for a moment, the frenzied feeding paused.

Mary circled, pinpointing the approaching anomaly, her instincts alerted to possible danger.

As was her way, Bloody Mary sounded and went low, disappearing into the deep darkness.

CHAPTER 27

"What do you mean, a boat's gone down?" Kate demanded. "What boat?"

Beside her, Lauren's eyes widened.

Kate kept herself deliberately calm, just as her mother had taught her. Her first thought when she saw Hendricks' number was that one of the protesters had done something crazy, like maybe charge one of the tugs – anti-whalers were known for that.

Or, God-forbid, had one of those piss-ant little protesters been hit by a shark?

Kate did a quick review of her liabilities. She wasn't stupid – anyone within a mile of this production had signed waivers. Kate had also made a point to legally cordon off the route – any civilian crossing the border was acting outside the law, and would therefore forfeit any potential damages.

Not that some of them might not sue anyway. Kate was already starting a slow burn at the thought – a *no-no*, her mother counseled – but then Hendricks interrupted.

"One of the tugs has been hit and gone down. And several civilian vessels. I'm looking for survivors now."

"One of the *tugs* is down? How? Hit by what? A shark?"

Kate exchanged bewildered looks with Lauren, who shook her head. No shark *alive* could damage a tug.

"No," Hendricks said, his voice shaking, "a *whale*."

There was a heartbeat of silence.

Midway through the south-tug's route was the one area where they had no live-feed.

But Hendricks was now sending her images on her phone.

Likewise, some of the surviving protesters' boats were also posting snippets of video.

The tug was a broken wreck.

Kate looked around the room. No one had yet noticed, and nothing had appeared on the big widescreens.

Then she saw Jerry, working his two phones and head-set, suddenly freeze, with one hand on his ear. Then his eyes turned grimly to the image on his phone. His face sober, he turned, eyeing Kate urgently from across the room.

The waitress-with-the-lower-back-tattoo was next, pausing to frown at her own phone, as she handed drinks to ferret-face and Blondie.

Liza had again separated Kenny from Lauren's chirpy little assistant, Nancy. Kate wasn't sure if it was jealousy or big-sister, but Liza deftly peeled Kenny's arm off the young girl's waist onto her own – and to be fair, Kate could see Nancy's heart puttering from over there – all of it on camera of course. That was the *reality* part of reality TV.

Currently, Liza and Kenny were wrapped over each other, staring out the window, posing in the aqua-blue light like lovers.

"Hey," Kate heard Kenny say. "Where'd all the sharks go?"

Outside, the sharks had suddenly vanished.

In the space of seconds, the frenzied pack scattered like a school of bait-fish.

All that was left was the murky unending blue, and the churning wake of the departing tugboat.

Nancy spotted it first. Frowning, she tapped Lauren's shoulder and pointed out the window.

"Doctor Palmer?" What does that look like to you?"

Materializing out of the misty blue, a massive shadow was rising.

Up from the depths...

Kate heard Lauren, her voice an awed whisper. "Oh my God."

They had a good clear view as a massive sperm whale came rocketing up from below.

It struck the tug in the right front center of the hull. The blow punched a hole larger than Kate's car.

Within the showboat, there was a mass, abbreviated gasp.

In moments, the tugboat was listing, and suddenly Kate's phone began beeping multiple numbers in her hand.

She still had Hendricks' line up.

"We've been hit," Kate said, as the full import now began to dawn.

The tug was sinking.

Here.

"Send help," Kate said, but even as she spoke, the tug was struck again.

Watching it through the poly-carbonate window reminded Kate of her first trip to Sea World as a child – the underwater view portals into the dolphin tank, where you could see them pumping their tails as they blasted towards the surface, launching clear out of the water like living water-rockets.

This was like that – a sixty-five ton dolphin with a head like a battering ram.

It hit the tug in the belly this time – the solar plexus just above the motor, rupturing the hull and spilling bubbling air like life-blood, as the guts of the heavy vessel flooded.

It seemed a deliberate move. In only two blows, the big boat floundered.

The showboat-screens blinked onto the image, parroted on clicking phones.

Looking out the windows, Kate could see the first kicking legs on the surface, as the crew was spilled into the water.

She felt Lauren grip her arm.

"We've got to get this boat over there. Get those men on-board."

But again, Nancy pointed, her breath hushed.

"*Look.*"

The massive shadow had appeared again.

Now it was coming right at *them*.

"Get on deck," Lauren said, curtly.

And then, obeying herself, she started to move, her hands grabbing both Kate and Nancy, dragging them along with her.

But it was too late.

Within the showboat, there was a moment of general confusion and abortive screams, as the massive beast bore down upon them like a titan.

The squared head hit the window dead-center, cracking the *unbreakable* alloy across the middle, and smashing it out of its frame. The hull of the showboat was smashed in with it.

In a flood, the ocean came pouring in.

CHAPTER 28

The lights in the showboat went dark.

Lauren was shoved and pushed roughly to the floor. Then she was tripped over, pinned and trapped, with the weight of five people piling down on top of her.

In bare moments, the room was flooded in icy water.

The initial surge of the crowd had been towards the stairs, but as its bowels filled, the boat rolled, and suddenly the crush against the stairs was tumbled blind and underwater.

Miraculously, the shift in weight and rush of ocean rolled the weight of the crowd off Lauren's back, and the smashed out window now loomed above as the only escape.

With barely a breath of air, Lauren kicked desperately for the light, even as she felt hands grabbing at her, trying to pull past.

This time, she kicked loose, defensively, slipping out into open water. Looking up, the surface seemed impossibly far away.

She felt the pull of the boat as it continued to roll in the water, dragging her back.

Trying to be calm, even as her lungs screamed and the world began to go dim, Lauren followed the light.

When her head broke the surface, she gasped air, and then choked, as the roll of waves threatened to slap her back under.

Nancy burst up with a splash, her eyes wide and panicked, followed by Kate, coughing and gasping.

Now there were screams and shouts as scattered survivors found their way to the surface.

Lauren saw Jerry Renner struggling, hurt and bleeding. Liza hovered close, treading water, helping keep his head up.

The showboat was half-submerged, held afloat by some interior air-pocket. Lauren saw no sign of crew, who had all been up top when the boat had upended.

Most of the tug-crew, however, had made their way on top of the floating mini-islands of whale carcasses, and now began pulling people out of the water.

There was no sign of Captain Blake, but Lauren saw his mate, shouting instructions, tossing ropes. He caught Blondie by the hand, yanking her up beside him, and then the waitress-with-the-lower-back-tattoo. Ferret-face sputtered up behind.

The two uncomfortably diminutive and already-overcrowded outboards tossed their equipment and began reaching for swimmers. Lauren saw the key-grip scrambling aboard.

Kenny had climbed atop one of the big female cachalots, and was currently fishing Nancy out of the water, pulling her up beside him.

Kate Foster had managed to haul herself up onto the back of the floating baby sperm whale, pulling herself by the snapped tether. She turned and waved to Lauren, who started paddling in her direction.

As she moved, she was suddenly aware of a swell underneath her feet – something large passing below.

Moving deliberately calm, fighting panic, Lauren reached for Kate's extended hand.

Kate anchored herself, and with a heave, she wrenched Lauren up onto the slippery carcass. Lauren felt her surprisingly strong grip, like a gymnast.

Liza and Jerry followed close behind – both of them laboring to keep Jerry afloat.

Once they got close, Jerry lunged forward, pushing away from Liza, reaching up.

At that very moment, he was hit.

The ocean exploded from below with nearly two tons of Great White shark.

Lauren recognized the markings and attack-style of Mack the Knife. The seventeen-foot male hit Jerry Renner in a full-on Polaris attack.

Lauren had filmed dozens of these attacks, almost all upon seals or decoys. It really didn't look that much different. Jerry wasn't a very big guy. His small form flapped in the shark's ragged jaws just like the baby seal.

Liza screamed as Mack crested, sailing completely overhead, before crashing back down, sending a wave up over the top of the floating baby cachalot, and nearly washing its riders back into the surf.

Lauren scrambled, latching onto the ropes. Kate reached out for Liza's hand.

Liza fought for purchase on the slick, rotting hide.

Right beside her, a steel-gray head, nearly three feet wide, rose up and took a bite out of the whale, leaving a two-and-a-half-foot hole.

On her other side, several more gray heads popped up like prairie dogs, lining the length of the carcass. Around and below, the ocean seemed to come alive as the frenzy begin to boil back up again.

The first of the conical gray heads turned with interest to Liza struggling in the water right beside them.

Lauren caught one of Liza's flailing hands, even as Kate grabbed the other. Together, they pulled her up beside them on the back of the floating baby whale.

Liza stared wide-eyed down at the water, roiling just below her feet like a blender with teeth.

She turned a sober eye to Lauren and Kate.

"Thank you," she said, sincerely, her voice barely a hiccupping whisper.

And then she slipped.

With a brief shriek, she slid like a water-slide, right into the middle of the reaching, straining maws.

Liza came up screaming, reaching wildly for the ropes.

As if in slow-motion, Lauren reached again for her outstretched hand.

In that brief, time-lapsed interval, Lauren caught another glimpse of those monster boobs.

But this time, she found she didn't have any trouble looking Liza in the eyes.

Lauren got a real good look at the desperate terror, as their hands missed each other, and Liza slid back down the baby whale's back into the water.

In fact, Lauren would remember it for the rest of her life.

Liza's head popped-up, briefly.

Then she was pulled back below and did not resurface.

Around them, the air erupted in screams.

Swimmers scrambled for floating wreckage, or up onto the backs of the tethered whales. Key-grip was directing his boat after stragglers who had started to drift in the current.

Lauren saw Cylvia Brown, clearly not a strong swimmer, clinging to a small floating donut, waving frantically.

Nancy had spotted her too, and was calling her name.

But it wasn't like they had a rope or a life-preserver they could throw her way.

It might not have made a difference, anyway, as she was picked off a moment later.

Not a Polaris-attack. The shark simply rose up and took Cylvia's small form, like snapping up flotsam on the surface. Lauren heard a short scream from Nancy.

There was not even a splash.

Lauren exchanged wide-eyes with Kate, who had the tethered rope wrapped around her wrist in a death-grip.

They felt a jarring tug, vibrating through the flesh of their small floating island, as it was savaged from below. Lauren wondered how long their sanctuary might last before it was literally eaten out from under them.

Three feet from her own curled toes, a silver-gray snout clamped its jaws into the blubber, chomping out one more beach-ball-sized chunk.

There was another eruption of water behind her, followed by accompanying screams.

Lauren turned her head, this time not even seeing who had been taken, just catching a splash and fins disappearing beneath the surface.

She saw the next one.

And the next.

Great White sharks have been compared to feeding trout, targeting twitching bugs at the surface.

This was a high-prey environment.

Survivors, clinging to wreckage and the backs of floating whales, watched helplessly.

Some phones were out, filming the carnage.

No doubt, the images were already going viral.

Even now, Lacey Chase's news-chopper was moving in above.

Lauren looked at Kate.

"So, how do you think the pay-per-view's doing *now*?"

Kate shook her head.

"I don't know. I lost my phone."

Lauren glanced down at her pocket.

She still had *her* phone. She pulled it out and tapped her screen alive.

"I wonder if Cody knows," she said. "I'll ask him."

CHAPTER 29

Cody had the live-stream image on his phone when Lauren's number popped-up in the middle of the screen.

As of yet, no one had cut the feed. There was live footage still coming in from every active camera, some still attached to half-sunken boats, and even the whales themselves – not to mention Lacey Chase, circling in her chopper, still reporting, now the sole-narrator of an internationally breaking-story.

One of the features on the pay-per-view feed, was the option to choose between any image, live on the network.

That option remained, even once people started being eaten.

The live images from underwater were quite graphic.

Cody glanced grimly at Pete and Tommy as he tapped Lauren's number. Her face appeared on his screen, wet and disheveled, with Kate hanging close over one shoulder.

"You're kidding, right?" Cody said. "How fucked are you *this* time?"

Lauren considered.

"Oh, *pretty* fucked. I'm sitting on a dead whale in the middle of the ocean. And right now, it's being eaten by sharks. Big sharks."

"Yeah," Cody said. "We're watching it live."

Lauren's haggard image on the tiny screen was particularly pathetic.

"Um. *Help?*"

Cody nodded.

"Honey, compared to our first date, this is easy. We're on our way."

Tommy was already turning them in the water, angling them back north before the motor even started.

Corky and the rest of the pod faded aside to let them through.

Pete looked back regretfully.

"Sorry, guys," he said. "But we've got a situation."

Corky swam up close again, chittering.

Cody was reminded of a dog he had as a kid, who had seemed to read his moods. Corky was clearly picking up on the alarm.

"You know," Cody said, "it was orcas that took out Big Rhonda." He glanced at Pete. "I don't suppose your friends might want to give us a hand?"

Pete and Tommy both shrugged. They *had* considered trying to lure in the off-shore pods.

"I'll ask," Pete agreed.

Now he leaned over the stern where the rest of the pod trailed.

"What do you say, guys?" He put his fingers to his lips and blasted off the piercing whistle he'd always used when it was time to head in from the bay.

The orcas recognized the call. And Cody was again reminded of his long-ago dog – once he'd gotten outside the yard, suddenly he didn't *want* to come when he was called.

Pete's whistle had the same effect – even Corky seemed to pull back a little.

No, I'm NOT coming back inside.

Pete shook his head.

"Seriously, guys," he called out to the hesitant grouping of black fins, "we could use your help here. I mean, this is what you guys *do*."

Pete nodded to Tommy.

"Go," he said.

Tommy pushed the throttle and *The Argonaut* lurched forward. Kate had helpfully informed them where *not* to be, so they knew right where to go.

About fifteen miles north.

The Coast Guard would already be on their way. Tommy had radioed in himself.

As if it was necessary – the live-feed had *started* global, and anyone even near the scene had been flooding the Guard's lines with calls.

But rescue still had to *get* there.

With the boats already policing the operation, they should be on-site within minutes. But to Cody's eye, those were some big minutes.

Cody hoped Lauren's floating whale held out that long.

Tommy clearly intended to get there as soon as *he* could. In moments, he took them up to speed, and had the big boat skipping like a jet-ski.

Cody looked back where they'd left Corky and her pod.

He realized the fins were in formation, moving along just behind them in their wake.

"They're following us!" Cody said.

Pete nodded, looking back.

Tommy gunned the throttle.

The orcas kept pace.

Tommy leaned over and touched the stereo. Over the speakers came a folksy rendition of *My Bonny Lies Over the Ocean*.

"Think she's around?" Pete asked.

"It's worth a try," Tommy said. "If Bonnie lost a calf, orcas are known to hold grudges."

Cody saw Pete's hand squeeze reflexively on his cane as he glanced back to the rag-tag fugitives that tailed along behind.

"For better or worse," he said, "that's very true."

CHAPTER 30

Corky led the pod after Pete, knowing full-well what they were headed into.

Humans were so foolish. This was not the first time Corky had found herself wishing Pete would simply leave well-enough alone.

To make matters worse, she could hear him calling out to *her* – the transient matriarch. By now, Corky knew her song, and what the humans called her.

Bonnie was not happy at Corky and her pod's continued presence in her waters.

Corky had been deft at avoiding the marauding transients – who, in the manner of orcas, were still more preoccupied with their daily-chores of finding food, than actually hunting them down.

And perhaps more than that, Bonnie was an experienced matriarch – she was content to let the disapproval she sent out in her sonar pings speak for her.

Ahab and Sandy, in particular, didn't like hearing *that* tone in the big orca-mama's voice.

Left to her own devices, Corky would have happily led them right along, possibly further south, completely out of Bonnie's migration range, as they attempted to establish a niche for themselves.

But *Pete* was still hanging around.

Corky could sense as well as any ocean-creature the perilous discord that stirred these waters.

It was even possible she recognized her own presence as an aggravating factor – again, another good reason to be on her merry way.

But there was Pete, running right into the middle of it.

It was his female – that *had* to be it – the woman who appeared at the facility that last couple of days – the one that seemed to activate Pete's own protective instincts.

If that was the case, she knew Pete wouldn't stop regardless of what waited.

But Corky was helpless even to warn him, beyond a series of urgent clicks and whistles.

Pete might not know what they were racing into, but Corky did.

There were things that could make even a killer whale afraid.

CHAPTER 31

Lacey Chase was still live. Circling above, her cameras recorded the whole thing.

Her live-stream feed also remained up. Because the incident was now a breaking-story, and the network already had exclusive rights, in the abrupt abdication of Jerry Renner, they had simply assumed producer's chores, switching the primary broadcast to Lacey's continuing commentary.

That did not, however, prevent subscription viewers from cutting to any image still being fed. The network made an unsuccessful attempt to block the particularly gory underwater shots – mostly after the fact. There wasn't anybody left still swimming.

When the whale attacked, the sharks had scattered, allowing most of the tug-crew to escape up onto the floating islands of blubber.

The showboat passengers were harder hit. They had still been in the water when the sharks regained their nerve.

Lacey couldn't have made an accurate count of how many had been taken.

Out of those that made it to the surface at all, after the boat rolled, Lacey had seen at least five separate breaches.

Each one of them had been shot at relative distance – but they were all clear enough to identify faces and names.

Other victims were simply snatched and pulled under. And there was no telling how many had been taken underwater, or simply drowned, trapped inside the sinking boat.

Lacey did the math – thirty VIP tickets sold – and by her eye, the tug-crew had fished out half that onto the backs of the tethered whales – none of the showboat's crew.

She wasn't sure how many film crew had been on-board.

The outboards had been crowded at five – one was now loaded at nine, the other at ten.

That was how many left that she *didn't* see?

Lacey had radioed both the police and the Coast Guard, who assured her help was on its way. They also informed her the second tug had been hit, and that the Guard was already on the scene.

She was firmly instructed to '*stay clear*' – that order relayed directly from Lieutenant Hendricks.

Lacey glanced over to her single pilot, whose badge identified him formally as 'Captain' Robert Wilson, but who she'd known for years as Bob.

"Take us in?" Bob asked.

Lacey wasn't sure what to do. It seemed ghoulish to just sit there and hover, filming people dying, but they had a two-person chopper. Beyond a couple of people possibly clinging to their landing gear, they were useless as a rescue craft.

For lack of options, Lacey simply kept filming.

She would be lying if she didn't recognize that she was being given the career opportunity of a life-time – a global audition.

And she needn't feel cynical. After all, Lieutenant Hendricks said help was coming. That meant they would soon be filming an inspiring rescue.

For the moment, the scene below looked to have calmed.

But as she looked closer, Lacey realized that wasn't really the case. There just wasn't anyone left struggling in open water.

She scanned all the different feeds on her console, including the live feeds from the underwater cameras.

There were the sharks, tearing away at the whale meat, and the floating islands were diminishing from the bottom-up, at an alarmingly rapid rate.

Impatiently, Lacey scanned the horizon for the Coast Guard. A chopper should be in the air.

But if they were already prioritizing the other wreck scene...?

How many rescue choppers capable of taking a load like this did they have?

At the rate the carcasses were being consumed, people were going to be back in the water again soon.

"Take us lower," Lacey said finally.

As if expecting the order, Bob dropped them down over the wreck-site.

The reverberating vibration of the chopper blades caused those clinging to floating whales to cinch up on their tether ropes.

One of the tug crew – it looked to be the mate – the one who Lacey had seen jumping from whale to whale, securing the ropes together, was waving her off.

Lacey nodded to Bob who edged them back.

Several of the carcasses had broken loose from the bunch, drifting precariously afar.

One of these was a calf, and as Lacey searched the crowd for faces, she recognized Kate Foster and Doctor Palmer perched on top.

Kate waved. Then she reached over and grabbed up Lauren's phone.

A moment later, Lacey's phone rang.

She tapped the screen and Kate's face appeared.

"Lacey, you need to back off. The vibrations are stirring up the sharks. They're starting to rock us."

"Do you want us to try and get you?" Lacey asked. "We can maybe get you on-board."

She heard Doctor Palmer in the background, "Oh *God*, no!"

"Listen, Lacey," Kate said. "Stay away from the surface, the whale's not gone..."

That was all she got out, because at that moment, Doby launched out of the water.

Lacey turned her camera down in time to catch the leap, as the massive squared head, came up at them like a breaching submarine.

It caught them flush, smashing their landing gear, and folding away the chopper's tail and rear rotors, sending the broken blades chopping deeply into the whale's broad head.

Doby thrashed angrily as he crashed back down into the ocean, sending up a wide plume of spray, along with waves that rocked the carcasses and the hapless passengers clinging to their backs.

When the whale struck, Lacey had time to scream, but the impact knocked her cold. She lay limp in the co-pilot's seat.

Bob struggled to control the damaged chopper with just the top rotors.

After several limping, wounded-crow spurts, the chopper piled into the sea.

Lacey's camera continued to record, right up until the last second.

Her final moments were already going viral – the massive monster rising up, the split of the narrow jaw and the rows of nine-inch teeth – then the moment of impact.

And then the spiral.

Finally, there was the flash of flame, as the chopper exploded.

CHAPTER 32

The chopper was recorded by multiple cell-phones as it careened across the sky and finally hit water – videos that all jumped at the point of impact, when the spinning rotor blades broke off into flying shrapnel.

The fiery blast momentarily startled the sharks.

Lauren had gone salmon-fishing as a kid and remembered her father instructing her to be very quiet while trolling, lest the sudden bumps scare the fish.

It was funny that Great Whites were like that too. At least, normally.

But apparently not today.

It was a matter of moments, not minutes, before the fins started circling again.

Kate and Lauren crowded together on the back of their slippery, fast-disappearing refuge. They were drifting away from the others.

Kenny and Nancy's whale had also broken loose and was following them into the current.

Belatedly, the tug-mate tossed a rope, but it fell short of Kenny's reaching hands.

There was nothing to do but wait. The Guard, the cops – all of them were on their way. They just had to *get* there.

Meanwhile, as each semi-circle chunk was bitten away, the carcass tugged and jostled, leaving Kate and Lauren scrambling on the slick hide.

There didn't seem to be a shark under sixteen-feet in the whole fuckin' ocean.

They exchanged baleful looks. At that moment, neither of them particularly liked the other, but they huddled close, nonetheless.

"It could be worse," Kate muttered. "It could be raining."

It was a strained attempt at a joke.

Unfortunately, Liza Carter's desperate face was still a little too vivid.

It could be worse, alright. Cue the lightning bolt.

And for a moment, as she heard a distant rumble, Lauren thought the incantation had actually worked.

Then she realized the sound was not thunder, but the drone of a boat-engine.

Accompanying that were the buzzing rotors of another chopper.

A slow cheer began to break out.

The tug-mate was standing and waving. Blondie and the waitress-with-the-lower-back-tattoo hooted and jeered. Key-grip, balanced haphazardly on an over-loaded outboard, held up a yellow life-jacket on the end of an oar. Kenny barked like a dingo, eliciting a squawk from Nancy as he slapped her water-soaked rump.

The Coast Guard had arrived. Or at least some of them. Lauren could see two boats motoring their way.

One of them was a coastal patrol boat – eighty-seven foot, marine-protector-class. Bigger than the tug Lauren had seen taken, but not a *lot* bigger.

The other was a good deal smaller – a thirty-foot port-security boat. That *had* to be Hendricks.

Kate still had Lauren's phone and now she tapped his number.

Hendricks answered, impatient.

"Lieutenant Hendricks. This better be good."

"It's pretty damned good," Kate shouted. "There's a whale!"

"Kate! Are you okay?"

"Not very!" Kate replied. "Are you listening to me? A whale did this."

"I know. I told you, I saw it take out the other tug." Then he glanced to someone off-screen. "It also hit several protesters. At least four dead."

"Leonard, listen to me. It's still here. The whale's still here. It took out the for-crissakes *news-chopper!*"

There was a pause, before Hendricks answered, his voice grim.

"We'll shoot it if we have to," he said. "Hold on a sec',"

They heard the crackle of static through the phone as Hendricks radioed the chopper.

"Gardner? You wanna pull up a bit? Like maybe out of range of a leaping whale?"

He tipped an eye back to his phone.

"And maybe keep a look-out for that big sonofabitch?"

"Will do, sir," Gardner replied, and above them, the chopper dutifully upped its altitude.

"And by the way," Kate said, "we're drifting out to sea on a whale carcass that's being eaten out from under us."

Hendricks came back on the screen.

"Yeah," he said, "I see you."

The smaller boat separated off to one side, circling the half-sunken wrecks and the tethered pilings of dead whales, even as the larger boat rumbled up slowly between them, clearly trying to avoid a wake.

The tug-mate waved them in. Lauren heard his heavy, workingman's drawl.

"Pretty happy to see *you* fellas."

But even as he spoke, the floating carcass rocked beneath his feet. The mate stumbled – Blondie and the tattoo-waitress both chirped, startled.

The tug-mate looked around warily.

Then the carcass was rocked again.

Fins and flapping tails slapped in the water.

This, Lauren thought, was not normal Great White behavior.

As the big patrol-boat bumped to a stomp, one of the guardsmen tossed down a ladder. The mate caught it, attempting to plant the metal-feet into the blubber, but the ladder slipped away into the water. Pulling it back, the guardsman tossed it out again.

Lauren waved at Hendricks as he came into clear view. She saw a sallow young woman, in tie-dyes and cutoffs, hunkered in the cabin beside him, looking wide-eyed and shell-shocked.

Hendricks recognized Lauren and waved back.

"Now where *else* would you be?" he said over the phone.

And because, for just the moment, she had begun to believe they might actually be rescued, Lauren allowed a moment of self-depreciation.

"Right in the middle of it," she agreed.

Then there was a muffled curse from Hendricks.

Lauren actually saw his thirty-foot boat shift in the water, like a car hitting a speed-bump.

Two sharks this time, knocking against the hull. Not enough to damage it, but still pretty damned unnerving.

"Jesus, they're being aggressive," Hendricks said. "I've never seen anything like this."

Lauren hadn't either. Not even with the charter boat.

On the other hand, no one had ever tried anything *this* stupid before.

Lauren took her phone back from Kate.

"You know, Lenny," she said, "I keep saying this, but you really need to get a bigger boat."

"We're kinda short-handed, all of a sudden," Hendricks replied. "We just evacuated an entire tug crew, and about five other boats."

"Who's the girl with you?"

"This here's Sally. She used to have four friends."

Lauren saw the girl dip her face into her hands.

"We sent the last boat to shore, filled to capacity. We also sent back two life-flight choppers. I'm hoping what we've got here is enough."

Hendricks pulled back, as he radioed the patrol-boat.

"Hey Rhodes, we've got two over-loaded outboards. You think they can make it to shore with an escort?"

"We'll get them there," Rhodes responded, "once we've picked-up everyone else."

"Then I'll get the drifters," Hendricks agreed.

Kenny and Nancy were closest, and he veered in their direction first.

Nancy's voice carried. "Oh, thank *God*."

And then, over the phone, Lauren heard the crackle of Hendricks' radio – Gardner from the chopper.

"I've got him, sir."

As if to announce himself, Doby spouted.

The spray erupted less than two-hundred yards out from where Lauren and Kate floated on the dead baby whale.

As Lauren looked down at the cachalot calf, it occurred to her for the first time that there might be a connection.

She looked up at the massive beast, circling like a shark.

"*Oh* boy," she breathed.

Hendricks shouldered his rifle and fired six shots in rapid succession. There was an answering barrage of gunfire from the top deck of the patrol-boat.

Lauren saw blood spurt from several spots across Doby's massive back. The big whale thrashed, throwing up spray, spouting in defiance.

"He's falling back," Gardner said.

"Stay on him," Hendricks said. "Keep him marked. If you get a safe shot, take it. And you let me know the second he tries to turn back around."

"Come on," he shouted, waving to Kenny and Nancy. "Let's get you all on-board and get the hell out of here."

But even as he said it, another shark hit the boat – *hard*.

"*Jesus*," Hendricks said, and now he raised his rifle.

The shark pulled away, thrashing in the water, as if frustrated at the lack of damage to its target. Even a big white couldn't sink a Coast Guard port-security vessel – not like a charter boat with a wooden motor-casing.

That did not, however, dissuade the pugnacious sharks from trying. A moment later, the boat was hit yet again.

Hendricks leaned over the side and fired a shot at one of the circling fins.

Remarkably, these sharks were not backing off.

Lauren had never seen behavior like this. Was it just the bait? Combined with numbers?

Then with sudden realization, she looked back to where Doby still hovered, barely three-hundred yards out,

Lauren recognized the pose, well-enough – the arched back, the splayed pecks, the big whale's own modest dorsal displayed seven feet above the waves.

He was posturing – demonstrating aggression. Challenge.

The circling sharks were responding with their own flayed fins and jerky side-to-side movements, poised to fight.

There was a sudden shout, followed by a curse from the tug-mate. He was still struggling to lash the ladder's metal-feet to the dead whale's thick hide, when they were again struck from below.

The shark that hit them actively tore at the carcass, almost as if trying to shake them loose. The mate pulled away, warning the others back.

Beneath their feet, the whale carcasses were being attacked. Not just bit – not just fed-upon – but *attacked.* Even the massive bulk of the big baleens shook with repeated impact.

Nancy shrieked alarmingly, latching onto both the tethers and Kenny's arm, as the whale beneath them was rocked.

Hendricks was within twenty-yards of them when they were hit.

Again, it looked like Mack the Knife – or perhaps Jabberjaw – but the shark hit with sufficient force to lift them in the water.

Nancy screamed again, clinging to the tattered ropes.

Kenny, however, was knocked over the side.

The sound he let out was not a scream so much as a bear-like howl, as he lurched back up the dead whale's slippery hide.

Nancy caught his hand, but his weight wrenched her own grip loose, and she toppled down on top of him.

They both splashed back down into the water.

Then, just as suddenly, they were both thrust upward again.

Lauren saw Nancy propped on Kenny's shoulders as a shark rose up beneath him, his leg clamped in its jaws.

Kenny's body was rigid, contorted in a frozen scream. Nancy caught a grip on a broken tether, even as Kenny's clasping hand grabbed hold of her foot.

Nancy kicked loose.

This time, Kenny let out something closer to a scream, as he was pulled under.

Nancy curled into a ball, clutching the rope, hiding her face and sobbing.

It happened in the seconds it took Hendricks' boat to travel twenty yards.

Now the Lieutenant reached down to her.

"Come on, girl," he said, calming. "We're going to get you home."

Behind him, sallow Sally suddenly stepped forward to help, reaching down for Nancy's other hand.

Gardner's radio barked again.

"He's starting to creep again, sir."

In the not-too-far distance, Doby blasted-off another spout.

Kate turned, covering her eyes in the sun.

"What's he doing out there? What's he waiting for?"

Lauren eyed the big whale. Doby was indeed holding back, perhaps respectful of the gunfire. But he wasn't retreating either.

Big male sperm whales were known to be stubborn. At least for the moment, he was holding his ground.

Hendricks reached down again for Nancy, who was nearly blinded by tears.

And at the moment their hands touched, they were struck.

Hendricks' boat was thirty-two feet long and solidly built. But the entire craft was picked-up cleanly out of the water.

In rapid succession, two more blows nearly split the bow in two.

Sally was catapulted several dozen yards, completely out of the boat, out into the ocean. Hendricks was rolled over on top of Nancy, and the dead whale, piling them both into the roiling water.

Behind the demolished boat, there was another spout and the unmistakable squared head of a sperm whale.

A moment later, two others answered, exhaling breath and breaching – all of them nearly-grown adolescent males.

The three of them continued to bump and slap the floundered security-boat with their massive tails.

There was immediate gunfire from the patrol-boat's tower.

A responding squeal pierced the air as one of the adolescents was hit. The thrashing whale sounded, followed immediately by its fellows.

Hendricks had found Nancy, knocked semi-conscious in the tossing surf, and he was trying to push her back up onto her perch aboard the dead whale.

But the sharks were already back.

Lauren had seen Sally hit the water limply, but now when she looked, the young woman's floating body was gone, taken in the moment it took to turn her head.

Hendricks and Nancy were surrounded by circling fins.

With a mighty heave, Hendricks latched onto one of the dangling ropes and shoved Nancy back up onto the dead cachalot. Nancy clutched the rope, grimly pulling herself up, hand-over-hand.

Hendricks was grabbed just as he tried to climb up behind her.

The shark came nearly three-feet out of the water – not a full-on Polaris-attack, but a good one-shot strike.

The jaws clamped shut, and Lauren heard a brief guttural grunt – *whoof* – like someone getting gut-punched and losing their air. Then the shark dropped back beneath the surface, dragging Hendricks with it.

Nancy let out a sob of utter despair as she clung desperately to the wet tether.

Lauren didn't clearly see what happened next.

She must have slipped.

Nancy uttered one brief screech, and then there was a small splash.

For a brief second, Lauren saw her head pop back up, but then she was promptly pulled below.

Just like that, she was gone.

Lauren's breath hitched in her chest.

She'd known Nancy for barely a year, and Lauren found herself remembering how she always followed along like a kid-sister, and how she seemed so *impressed* with *Doctor* Palmer – and how *irritating* she always was.

Lauren felt the sting of tears as she remembered how hard Nancy always tried to please.

And how hard she had tried to live, right there at the end.

Meanwhile, instead of being rescued, Lauren and Kate were now drifting off to sea, the buoyancy of their floating refuge more compromised with each passing second.

Behind them, Doby spouted again.

Opposite the wreck of Hendricks' boat, the adolescents answered with spouts of their own.

Doby reared up in the water, crashing down with a crescendo.

When he surfaced, he was moving toward them again.

CHAPTER 33

Lauren saw the great whale coming, the rising swell of ocean as intimidating as any dorsal fin – it was simply a *mass* – a charging sea-monster.

Release the Kraken.

"He's headed right for us," Kate said breathlessly.

The sharks parted and gave way, clearing Doby's path, but didn't scatter – *they* were not the target.

Lauren felt the ocean rise up. Kate let out a low moan as they braced for impact.

But instead, the great whale ducked under the floating calf, and surged past.

Lauren turned, watching the huge shape rocket by underwater.

Doby was charging the eighty-seven-foot patrol-boat.

Approaching from under the tethered carcasses provided him cover from gunfire.

The big whale hit the boat underwater. Lauren couldn't see the impact, but the entire vessel shuddered.

She heard a voice on-board shout in alarm.

"Jesus. He's punched a hole in us!"

It would be the third boat of its general size Doby had sunk today. He was developing technique.

He charged underwater again. The boat itself seemed to recoil.

Above, Gardener brought the chopper in close. A man with a rifle leaned out the side, hunting for a target.

Then there were three staccato BOOMS, as the adolescents followed Doby, taking turns bashing the big boat's hull.

The bow flooded, and the patrol-boat started to sink.

The guard-crew was now faced with rescuing themselves, and the six instead of four-man crew, now meant more seats in a lifeboat.

It was ironic, in a way, that a rescue-boat *had* a life-raft. Unfortunately, it was of the rubber sort. Lauren saw the crew pushing it over the side, automatically inflating.

Worse, the tug-mate had now just secured the ladder to a rapidly-sinking hulk, that was also starting to pull away – he had already started sending his people across.

The mate grabbed the waitress off the bottom rungs, pulling her back, but Blondie was already stretched out over the water, and as the ladder turned, she started to fall.

Her voice rose in a scream before the mate caught her arm, heaving her back with a grunt, toppling them both over the waitress and nearly knocking them all off the other side.

Ferret-face had nearly made it over the railing, but now found himself perched atop the floundering patrol boat. One of the guardsmen reached for him and, for a moment, looked as if he had him, but instead he plopped ten feet, right into the circling fins. He never resurfaced.

The tug-mate cut the ladder away. But the sharks' relentless assault was taking its toll on their group of floating islands. The ropes that lashed the carcasses together were starting to stretch apart.

Realizing what was happening, the mate shouted to the others.

"We've got to pull them together!"

But before he could move, Doby came up from underneath.

The giant cachalot rose up between them, tearing the tethered ropes apart.

It was impossible to tell who, but at least half-a-dozen bodies went flying as the monster whale breached.

Any screams were drowned in the deluge as Doby crashed back down into the ocean, straps of tattered, tangled line dragging behind.

Lauren saw the tug-mate clutching Blondie as they both clung to broken lashings.

The waitress had been washed over, but Blondie caught her hand, and with the mate's help, hauled her back up.

A half-second later, a shark slammed against the whale, right in the spot where she'd been.

The Guard's rubber life-boats were launched, but there was a sudden gunshot explosion as one of the pontoons burst under a chomp from two-foot jaws. There were mixed shouts as the punctured raft immediately started to sink.

The outboards were next

Perhaps the sharks were following Doby's lead, or maybe they were just hyper-activated – or it was possible they were just simply really big fish that had once-and-for-all lost any fear of boats.

Key-grip's over-loaded outboard was first. Lauren heard his voice rise hysterically – "Oh, holy SHIT!" – as water came rushing in from a hole bit into the stern.

Again, it looked like Mack the Knife. But it was difficult to tell. They were *all* acting out – an elevated crowd-response.

You couldn't even fairly call their behavior unpredictable, because they were reliably biting anything that moved.

Key-grip screamed as the outboard flipped, and dumped the crowded boatload into the surf. Key-grip was pulled under in moments.

Then the second outboard was hit. Screams rose again, and the tug-mate made an effort to toss a rope their way. But there were simply too many teeth – no one who went into the water lasted more than a minute.

The sharks were actually breaching. Just like trout.

Lauren and Kate had gotten a brief reprieve when Doby had scattered the sharks from their own mini-flotsam, especially now that they were drifting away from the main frenzy.

But Lauren felt the first tug as the scavenging jaws returned.

The remains of the calf were now only a few feet above water. Soon the carcass would start to sink under their weight.

They had another few minutes at best. She wondered passingly if Kate would try to kick her off first.

And then suddenly, the sharks feeding beneath their feet again dropped back below the surface and vanished.

Just as suddenly, the circling fins also disappeared.

In the space of seconds, the roil of the water abruptly ceased, settling into an eerie calm.

Lauren heard an approaching motor.

Coming from the south was *The Argonaut*.

Surrounding it, were the tall black fins of orcas.

"Oh my God," Kate breathed, "he found them."

She cast a chagrined eye at Lauren and the remaining flotsam of their whale.

"He may be a bastard, but he *does* show up."

Lauren was thinking the same thing almost verbatim about Cody.

This was twice now. Was it still because of Carson, she wondered?

Although perhaps a better question might be, what was to stop the same thing from happening to *The Argonaut* that happened to both tugs, the Guard, and the showboat?

Were Pete's pet orcas going to fight off that big cachalot? Not to mention, all three adolescents?

But as Lauren looked over her shoulder, she saw Doby holding his distance.

The big whale was covered in scars, but there were a number of pretty nasty wounds that looked recent.

And while Doby seemed to allot the rogue pod a healthy respect, he was not ceding ground.

Lauren remembered the torn-out tongues on the beached sperm whales – the same injuries on both females, and the calf that she rode upon now.

Was Doby now faced with the orcas who had killed them? The ones who had given him those fresh scars?

And was he now backed-up by three nearly-grown adolescents?

Perhaps Doby was still trying to decide that himself, because he continued to patrol, spouting at the perimeter. The adolescents had retreated further back.

Lauren's phone rang. Cody's number.

She picked up.

Cody didn't waste a beat.

"You owe me, big-time, after *this*," he said.

Lauren shut her eyes.

"You know," she said, "you signed off on this. This is your fault too."

Kate narrowed her eyes, but said nothing.

"That's kind of a reach," Cody replied.

Lauren started to answer, something brave, and quippy, and flip.

Instead, she teared-up.

"It's good to see you, Cody," she said.

There was half-a-tick as Cody heard her tone.

"Hang tight, ladies," he said. "We're gonna get you."

Lauren felt her stomach lift with the swell of the ocean, as the first of the towering black fins sailed by. The drooping fin of an older male veered close, like a dog running by for a passing sniff.

The pod circled the floating carcasses, and the pitiful humans perched on top.

Lauren saw the tug-mate, clinging to both the waitress and Blondie as the massive black-and-white shapes glided past, unsure if they were seeing salvation or just another monster.

The orcas circled the perimeter with military efficiency, cruising between the dead whales, and the junkets of semi-submerged wrecks.

The big female that seemed to be leading the pod circled back in front of the approaching *Argonaut*, as if to confirm the area was secure.

In eye-distance now, Cody waved from the deck.

"We've got you, honey," he said in Lauren's ear.

But behind her, there was another blast of air, as Doby spouted belligerently at the perimeter.

The adolescents were still tentative, but Doby seemed to be posturing up.

For the moment, he was held at bay.

But he continued to circle, subtle as a shark, edging ever closer.

CHAPTER 34

As Tommy drifted *The Argonaut* gently forward, Cody rooted around his pack and produced a thin tin canister, like a beer-can with a pull-top.

He turned a quick eye to Pete, who nodded, and Cody pulled the tab, tossing the fizzing canister into the surf.

This was the 'scent-of-death' – that same remarkably effective shark-repellent that had worked for him in his last close-scrape with agitated Great Whites.

The stench was awful, specifically designed to highlight elements of rot. It was ironic – sharks did not like the smell of their own dead – creatures that lived on death, followed it, scented it out for miles. Yet in multiple field tests, time after time, sharks of different species were shown to vigorously retreat from the released chemicals.

These were the last two canisters he'd had at home. He held the second in reserve.

"You know," he said, waving the can at Tommy, "with all your funding, it'd be a good idea to get a lot of this stuff."

"Yeah," Tommy agreed, his attention focused on his steering. "Too bad no one brought it up until just this morning."

Cody leaned over the rail, watching the canister spin.

The sharks *seemed* to have scatted at the intrusion of the orcas, but there was nothing wrong with putting a little pepper on it.

It *was* an effective chemical after all – the only drawbacks being that it had to be same-species.

And, of course, all those currents, that would quickly wash the scent away.

"Think they're gone?" Cody asked.

"I doubt it," Pete said. "But maybe they'll lay low for a minute."

"That big whale's posturing," Tommy said.

He nodded over the railing where Corky and Orky rode their wake, positioned like offensive blockers, as Doby circled the perimeter.

"Think your friends can take him?" Tommy asked.

"I think," Pete replied slowly, "they've taken at least one shot at it already."

Tommy nodded. "Yeah. And I think he remembers."

Doby spouted once again. Sperm whales were known to spend ten to twenty minutes breathing between dives.

Now, it seemed he was ready again.

The big whale turned in their direction.

Corky and Orky immediately veered to intercept.

Tommy whistled through his teeth.

"This is going to get rough," he said.

Corky and Orky were both big animals – fast and powerfully-built, but at a glance, both of them together were woefully inadequate to the living dreadnought that had now kicked its massive flukes in a full-on charge.

Cody was startled by a shot from above, as the chopper circled.

Doby ignored the bullets, bearing down on the two smaller whales.

Then he was suddenly struck from below.

Ahab's fin appeared as the big transient rolled in the water, following up his charging attack to the great whale's ribs with a heavy tail-strike at the huge, domed head.

Doby shrugged off the impact, charging past, only to have Sandy strike from the other side.

Old Skipper, who'd seen his better years, was still a huge Antarctic type, drooping fin and all – he careened up from below into Doby's stomach.

Now Orky and Corky split to either side, and as the big cachalot attempted to charge past, the two cheeky resident-orcas latched onto his pectoral fins.

Merry and Pippin both followed, chomping their scissor-jaws on the flukes.

"I'll be damned," Tommy said. "They got this."

Doby thrashed away from the clinging orcas, twisting in the water and sounding.

Orky and Corky circled back to the surface, joined a moment later by Ahab, Sandy, and the Skipper, resuming their defensive perimeter around the boat.

Doby surfaced again, less than a hundred yards out.

Bleeding and battered, he still had not yet had enough.

Circling behind him were the three adolescents.

To Cody's eye, their participation in the fight could make a big difference.

But he also suspected the three fledgling bulls were orphaned for a reason. For the moment, they still held back.

Doby spouted, his back arched and threatening.

The big cachalot wasn't waiting.

He turned again, readying for a charge.

The rest of the rogue orcas filed in, reinforcing the line-up. Merry and Pippin joined Annie and Mary, circling the ship. Doc, Happy and Dopey – big pack-ice orcas – moved in behind Ahab and Sandy like line-backers.

Big ol' Skipper faced Doby down the middle like a nose guard.

The big cachalot took full measure of his foes.

Cody wondered what was going through the animal's mind?

It appeared to be gearing-up for what amounted to a suicide run.

In Cody's experience, animals didn't just *do* that. Nothing was stopping it from simply fleeing the scene.

For whatever reason, this particular whale had decided to go down swinging.

And but for the failing-nerve of a bunch of frightened adolescents, the big cachalot might have had the fire power to pull it off.

By himself, Cody thought Corky and her pod had his measure.

This time, however, the threat for the orcas came from below.

CHAPTER 35

As was her nature, Bloody Mary circled in the depths below the rest.

Having been drawn out into open ocean, when the orcas had appeared, the sharks had retreated deep. A completely instinctive response, much different than miming Doby's posing displays.

But now the chemical – the *scent of death* – had been introduced into the water.

Again, the reaction was instinctive – instant panic – instant flight.

But right at the moment, there were just too damn many of them.

With their every olfactory sense warning them of threat, and their reflexive instincts telling them to flee, finding that flight blocked, left no option but to lash out at everything at once.

Saw-toothed jaws snapped, as they clashed in the darkness, thrashing side-to-side, in invisible posturing.

In such an environment, Rhonda once would have done the heavy-lifting. Things were so much easier then.

It now fell to Mary to establish dominance.

And she saw her primary rival, the harlequin-shape, silhouetted at the surface – the white belly, open and vulnerable.

Mary perceived the tide of the battle that had been raging above, and knew Doby had taken his lumps.

She also recognized the reluctant presence of the orphaned adolescents, who might change things.

A fish like Mary had an extremely primitive brain – there was no predetermined plan to her movements. Yet, how often did animal instinct seem to mimic strategic thought?

And how many times throughout history have two armies stood at swords points, hovering on edge, on unending pause, until that first strike – the first arrow, the first slash of the sword – lit the fuse, and in an instant, one became ALL?

Doby was building up steam for his final run, but Mary could see that the rogue pod of orcas had his number.

In Doby's position, Mary would have long since retreated, down to the deepest crevices where the air-breathing orca simply couldn't go.

Mary had no idea why Doby would behave in such a manner, nor did she have the ability to question it. Instead, she simply acted on the opportunity it afforded her.

She zeroed in on the pod's structural center – the nose guard – the big male with the drooping fin – old Skipper.

In the space of seconds, Bloody Mary came shooting up out of the darkness – up from the depths – and always from behind.

Backed by over two-and-a-half tons, her jaws slammed into the old male orca at the base of his tail – right where Rhonda had hit the gray whale calf, and the orca calf after that.

Where Megalodon had once targeted whales for its daily diet.

Mary was getting big enough.

Her strike was unguarded and clean, her teeth carving through flesh into bone.

There was an outraged squealing as the big orca thrashed in the water, its massive body twisting like a five-ton tentacle, flapping its big pectoral fins, reaching back angrily with his teeth.

The big shark took a glancing blow as she pulled back quickly, out of range.

But Mary knew she had scored a telling hit. Her jaws had cleaved away nearly three-feet of tail-fluke and bone.

The Skipper was now crippled.

With her mouthful of meat, bone, and blubber, Mary dived, headed back down deep.

As was her way – retreat once the fuse was lit.

CHAPTER 36

There was something particularly horrible about the scream of an orca.

It was like the agony of a child, yet at the same time eerily non-human, like a squealing pig.

The Skipper was hit from below and from behind. Pete clearly saw a HUGE shark, easily twenty-feet – nearly the size of an average adult orca by itself.

As the Skipper thrashed, the other orcas actually seemed taken aback.

The shark, one-hit ambush predators that Great Whites were, vanished immediately after the strike, retreating before the rest of the pod could respond.

Skipper rolled in the water and as his tail broke the surface, the wound became visible.

Pete grimaced. He heard Cody beside him, "*Jesus.*"

The Skipper's moans of pain carried on the air.

There was a brief pause, as they all absorbed the new way of the world.

The attack had broken the orcas' front-line – taken out their nose guard.

Uncharacteristically taken by surprise, they weren't reacting well.

Their first attention went to the Skipper, as Merry and Pippin moved to hold him up. Ahab and Sandy both covered point, facing off Doby, who was still bristling, threateningly.

But they hadn't yet adapted to the suddenly emboldened sharks that were now rising up from below.

There was yet another squealing scream as little Orphan Annie was hit.

Barely sixteen-feet herself, the attacking shark was bigger than she was.

This time, the strike was not targeted at the tail, but at center mass. Annie was killed on impact.

Finally, the pod responded, abandoning the surface, engaging the gray torpedo shapes underwater, where sonar outlined their presence, and they could now spot the big sharks coming.

Pete could see massive shapes zooming back and forth beneath the waves.

The water actually seemed to *churn*.

In ninety-nine out of a hundred cases, Pete would give an orca pod a decided advantage against any number of sharks, but these were BIG Great Whites, and they were badly out-numbered.

The orcas' approach was to take the offensive. The first shark-casualties were immediate and brutal.

The shark that hit Annie was not quite so quick in its retreat, and it was set upon before the spray of the attack had settled.

Marty hit the shark sideways. It was another big female, over eighteen-feet, and it lurched back towards Marty's face with extremely formidable jaws of its own, but was caught completely unawares as Merry and Pippin slipped up behind and flipped the shark on its back, inducing tonic immobility, allowing Marty to tear open the belly.

It was a technique orcas often used against sharks all over the world. The whales who practiced it, were deft, working together, so they rarely got bit.

But this time, there were a lot more sharks. And these orcas were learning on the fly.

Pippin was forced to release his hold as he was hit by yet another attack. The shark again targeted the tail, but Pippin sensed its approach, twisting like a seal at the last second, so the teeth only glanced his flukes – whereupon the big orca spun around and smashed those same heavy tail-fins across the shark's conical head. Merry's tail bludgeoned down as well, before Marty once more charged in, latching his teeth into the shark's gills, and tearing them out.

But the shadows below were becoming ever bolder. The initial assault on the Skipper seemed to have broken a mass psychological barrier.

And that was not the only problem.

Doby had paused on the old Skipper's scream, a sound he had likely never heard before.

It apparently gave him renewed confidence. The massive beast ceased its pacing and launched forward.

Confidence, it seemed, was catching.

Skulking the far-perimeter, the largest of the adolescents now breached. Fifty-feet of cachalot cleared the water.

Pete was reminded of a big ape, tearing-up the bushes, as it worked up steam for a head-on attack.

The adolescent hit the water and, with a pump of its flukes, it charged.

"You know," Tommy said, "we might be in trouble."

After a moment, the other two adolescents breached, following their brother.

"Definitely," Pete replied. "Definitely in trouble."

The orca pod was already down two members. Annie floated lifelessly and the Skipper floundered helpless, as the others were forced to defend themselves from the marauding sharks.

Pete saw several silver-gray fins circling the big orca but, for the moment, the Skipper was holding them off.

But he was no good in the fight. On a normal day, the pod would have been duly challenged to take on Doby himself, let alone in the big cachalot's current frame of mind.

Now as the adolescents approached...?

And there were still far too many sharks – none of them a threat to a cachalot, but just big enough for an orca.

In bare minutes, it seemed the battle had turned quickly south.

By Pete's estimate, they were going to simply be overwhelmed.

Which, he realized, likely meant any lingering boats that dared remain afloat would quickly follow.

Then he felt Cody's hand on his shoulder.

"Pete. Look."

Tommy whistled through his teeth.

As they turned to the east, it was as if the entire ocean was suddenly filled with tall black fins.

Pete couldn't have guessed a number. But he recognized Bonnie and her transient-pod – numbering at least thirty.

But bringing up the rear was Calypso – matriarch of an off-shore pod of over two-hundred.

"I've never seen this before," Tommy said. "Never in my life. These pods don't cooperate. They don't even interact. This is unprecedented."

Cody eyed the sudden armada of towering black dorsals nervously.

"What's about to happen here?"

"Well," Tommy said, "if we were talking about humans, I'd say *war*."

He glanced at the aligned forces – the rogue pod, the charging cachalots, the schooling, frenzied sharks.

"Here, right now, today?"

Tommy shrugged and then nodded.

"I'd say, yeah. That."

CHAPTER 37

The death cry of a killer whale had activated something in the mama orca's brain.

Bonnie could not have articulated what had truly drawn her to this place today – nor the inexplicable presence of Calypso, arriving in her numbers.

The big off-shore pod had just suddenly *been* there, identifying themselves only at the very last with their signature clicks – sneaking-up, as off-shore pods tended to do.

Ordinarily, that would have been a sanctionable breach of etiquette. There had already been skirmishes between the eco-types this season, over just such transgressions.

Of course, that had been before they had identified the presence of the rogues.

Bonnie had known they were still in the area. Their dorsals, so to speak, had surfaced by making contact with the humans – the ones who played the songs.

The orca matriarch also suspected the reason the leader of the rogue pod had decided to make themselves known.

It seemed that many things were happening that had never happened before, and would have to be dealt with.

Other priorities had surfaced that would have to trump etiquette.

The *why* of it was simple enough. A dead killer whale with a shark bite in it.

Another orca had been killed by a Great White, off the very same coast as her own calf. And a third had been attacked.

To call Bonnie's response territorial was not wrong, but in the case of orcas, it was possible they realized something more was at stake.

A territorial dispute could be resolved as such things had in the past, by simply running trespassers off the hunting grounds.

This was a shift in ecological power – the setting of a precedent.

Aided and abetted, of course, by those meddling humans.

It was important, in Bonnie's world, that the Great White response to orcas remain the *instinct-to-retreat*.

She had thought she'd done her part, after Big Rhonda had killed her calf. Obviously, there was more to do.

Today, however, that was Calypso's job. The off-shore pods were the shark-killers. Today was a day to let the specialists do their work.

Bonnie's job was Doby.

Taking down big whales was what transients did.

The big matriarch paused as her pod conjoined with the rogues' battered defensive line.

Bonnie approached Corky as she and Orky maintained a defensive posture in front of the human's boat.

Corky rose to meet her – by orca standards, the harlot with the scarlet letter – saddled with a hybrid lovechild.

Ahab and Sandy, the two big transients that traveled with them, hung attentively on Bonnie's every movement and posture.

The male, Bonnie knew, would have been the sire.

Bonnie and Corky touched noses briefly.

All *that* was for later.

For the moment, there were other priorities.

The two of them turned, big mama and big sister, as the orcas braced, forming a line, as the giant cachalots came bearing down.

CHAPTER 38

Lauren had never seen anything like it.

The orca fins shifted into factions – the taller, sharper fins of the transients turning to engage the cachalots, while the smaller, round-tipped fins of the off-shore pod moved in and began targeting sharks.

The dwindling refuge of the whale-calf had been nearing its practical end, with Lauren and Kate both clinging to what was left of the broken tethers, but they were granted extra minutes as the feeding sharks turned to engage the orcas.

While the rough chop only allowed brief snapshots of what went on below, the water was clear, and Lauren could see enough.

The sharks did most of their damage in kamikaze moves.

Lauren recognized their jerky, twitching movement, and in a way she actually found herself sympathizing. What she was seeing was sensory haywire – massive amounts of overloaded, and contradictory stimulus.

The panicked sharks were reacting the only way they were capable – they were biting anything in reach – even each other.

Lauren recognized the jagged fin of Mack the Knife, charging directly into the path of the smallish off-shore orcas – not even in ambush, but an all-out, frontal assault. He actually got his teeth into an unwary male, delivering a vicious bite on the face, nearly taking an eye, before Calypso herself latched onto the big shark's gills and the other pod members moved in to tear Mack apart.

Circling above the wreck, Gardner dropped the chopper back down into range. They lowered a rope ladder, and the tug-mate held it steady, waving to the others. The guardsman in the chopper was no longer shooting, but kept a watchful eye.

And now, *finally,* Lauren heard the drone of more choppers.

Kate covered her eyes in the sun, trying to see.

"I think at least one of those is Navy." She nodded to the still-live image on Lauren's phone. "Maybe the president's watching."

Lauren blinked at the thought. It had not occurred to her that they might actually still be live. But glancing down at her phone, sure enough.

The tug-mate ushered both Blondie and the waitress up the ladder onto the hovering chopper – full to capacity at six-deep. They looked worriedly back at the others, as the whirling-bird lifted. The mate waved them on, pointing at the incoming choppers on the horizon.

By Lauren's measure, their own rescue was minutes away.

She and Kate, however, would be counting those minutes in seconds.

The Argonaut was drawing near. Cody held up a rope, ready to throw the second they were close enough.

Doby, however, picked that moment to break through the orcas' front line.

Ahab and one of the wild transient males were roughly knocked aside. Orky made a desperate attempt to latch on to the charging cachalot's passing pectoral fin, but the big resident male was tossed brutally, his five-tons sent tumbling.

With the way clear, Doby charged *The Argonaut.*

At the helm, Tommy turned to face him.

Lauren and Kate watched helplessly, as Tommy gunned the throttle, revving up like a drag engine, spinning the sixty-foot boat like a jet-ski, as if he intended to meet the charging beast head-on.

What the hell was he *doing*?

Was it *ego?* Lauren wondered. She had time to think that was *just* like a man, and that this bit of go-out-on-your-shield bravado was going to get them *all* killed.

Doby certainly seemed to think so. The giant cachalot practically snorted blood as it targeted its mark.

Lauren almost covered her eyes as the two charging opponents closed – a tick of a second before Tommy yanked the wheel and touched them deftly aside, like a surfer hopping waves.

The monster whale hurtled past. The boat took only a slight impact as it scraped Doby's hide and caught a single passing blow from the mighty tail.

Unfortunately, that now left Lauren and Kate directly in Doby's path.

This time there was no avoiding it

The final seconds before impact seemed to drag.

As Doby bore down, Lauren turned away, and as she did so, she happened to catch Kate's expression, rooted on the charging whale, absolutely focused, nothing else on her mind.

In that odd, brief interlude, Lauren had time to think that she and Kate were different that way – Lauren didn't want to see it coming.

She shut her eyes.

But she felt the impact just the same.

The carcass beneath them was struck and Lauren felt herself flying. She opened her eyes to a spinning sky, and water *way* too-far down below.

After a nauseatingly slow, tumbling arc, Lauren's momentum crested and she began to fall back towards the water.

When she hit, she plunged down deep. Stunned by the stinging impact, she found herself nearly blind in the dark.

But as her eyes adjusted, she saw large indistinct shapes moving all around her. She could feel the displaced water of their passage.

Lauren felt a cold pulse of terror.

Her air was gone. She began to kick for the light above.

She knew the last ten feet to the surface was the death-zone in white-shark waters.

It was knowledge that mattered not at all, as she kicked desperately, bursting through the surface, and gasping a desperate breath.

As she was lifted by the energetic swells, she saw Kate – thrown nearly forty yards, knocked completely in the opposite direction.

They were both now swimming out in the open ocean.

Kate suddenly screamed, and Lauren saw the water rise up underneath her.

In the next moment, she was sitting on the black and white dome of Corky's head.

Dropping briefly below, Corky slid forward until Kate got a purchase on her dorsal.

Turning deftly, Corky circled back towards *The Argonaut*.

With Kate on her back, and in a move she must have performed on stage a thousand times, Corky rose up quickly next to the rear deck.

Pete caught one of Kate's arms, and Cody the other, and they snatched her deftly off the orca's dorsal and on-board.

Kate stood unbelieving, her eyes blinking salt-water.

"I know," Pete said, "your lawyers say I'm not supposed to be this close."

"I'd've let them *eat* her," Tommy shouted, as he cranked the wheel.

Cody was pointing after Lauren.

A half-step ahead, Orky was already circling in her direction.

It was however, something much larger than an orca that rose up in the water beneath her, as Lauren attempted to paddle towards rescue.

Suddenly, she was sitting on a living island of muscle.

"Oh my God...," she murmured, even as her hands found grips on the broken tethers tangled across Doby's massive back.

Lauren clung like a fishhook as the great whale cut through the water – sixty-five tons, breaking the waves like a living U-boat.

Then the mighty cachalot breached.

He dipped briefly below the surface, before leaping straight up, cresting his massive weight, hanging suspended for one impossible moment, his full seventy-feet completely clear of the water.

Then, with the cascading slow-motion of an avalanche, he crashed back down beneath the surface, and dived.

CHAPTER 39

Lauren was nearly torn away as Doby hit the water. The shock rattled her teeth, almost knocking her out.

If he had landed on his back, she would have been smashed like an insect.

As it was, semi-conscious, her only thought was to take a breath, because now he was going under.

Lauren's strength was fading by the second. She was simply unequal to the torque of water-pressure against sixty-five tons of rampaging cachalot, as Doby dove down past the fading light.

But she couldn't let go if she wanted to – her hands clenched the tethers like wrapped wire.

She was about to drown, *before* the pressure in her head burst her skull.

Carson had done this once, on the back of a humpback.

It hadn't been pissed off, but it had taken her deep.

Lauren hung as limp as a rag – except for her fingers, locked in a frozen death-grip.

Then suddenly she was aware of wind instead of water cutting her face, as Doby broke the surface – breaching once again.

Lauren rose with him, a bug on his back, riding the leviathan like a jockey.

She felt them cresting – ten stories high.

As they began to tumble, Lauren caught a glimpse of the boat – so far below.

She took the opportunity to scream bloody murder.

And then, from her rapidly-descending vantage, as the cachalot came crashing back down, she also saw the black-and-white shapes of pursuing orcas.

Lauren caught her breath, bracing for the underwater drag, but this time the big whale was back on the surface in a moment, racing the perimeter.

As she looked over her shoulder, Lauren saw orcas on both sides – big transients, porpoising in their wake.

And just behind *them*, charging like the front line in a stampede of cattle, were all three adolescents, each with their own entourage of orcas mugging them on all sides, snapping at their fins, bumping and ramming their sides, pushing them underwater.

Lauren looked over Doby's broad back as the big bull's own black-and-white assailants moved in.

She felt Doby tense, ready to fight.

Lauren took a breath, cinching her grip, ready to hang on for her life.

As the orcas closed, Doby dove.

This time it was several minutes before they surfaced again.

When she finally felt air, Lauren screamed again.

"HELP ME!"

They charged along at surface-level, the surge of waves off the whale's back pulling at her like a leaf on a windshield.

The orcas were not helpful in that regard.

Lauren felt the first impact all the way through Doby's ribs.

The gasping spout exploded in front of her, followed by sucking wind, loading oxygen.

The big cachalot was preparing to go deep this time.

If he took her down into the chasm, for Lauren, it would be over.

But this time, when he arched into his dive, he found more orcas waiting for him, striking immediately from below, knocking away his air, and forcing him back to the surface.

Doby's response to this strategy was the same as when he broke through their line to attack the boat – pure physical force.

Lauren felt Doby gathering himself, coiling sixty-five tons of torque.

She took a breath as he dipped briefly below the surface, gathering momentum, and then she held-on with the last of her fading strength as the great whale reared up in yet another dramatic breach.

Lauren felt herself loft, riding a centrifugal force of who-knows how many tons?

They crested at over a hundred feet.

Then Doby began to fall back towards the water, and this time he was turning, corkscrewing onto his back.

Lauren realized he was going to land on top of her.

She saw it – and in the second she saw, she acted.

When she felt the momentum shift, in that pause before gravity reclaimed her, she let go of the tethers, and simply leaped into wide open air.

There was a brief, stomach-dropping moment where she seemed to hover. As a little girl, when she had taken elevators in tall buildings, she always leaped, right at the moment the car stopped, feeling the sudden momentum-shift seemingly propel her into the air. It made her mother nervous, she remembered, suggesting it wasn't the safest thing for the elevator cables.

It was that same half-moment of float that she doubled back to now, as she simply launched herself out into space.

Lauren tumbled in the air like a cat, struggling to see which way was down – how FAR was down.

As she began to fall, she oriented herself feet-first towards the ocean.

Carson would have pulled it, Lauren knew. She would have made it look easy. She would have posed like a ballerina, and cut the water without a splash.

Lauren didn't make it look easy.

Falling awkwardly, she hit the water like a rock.

She was aware of impact. Then there was a momentary blackness.

The next thing she was aware of was floating limply on the surface.

Just a loose piece of flotsam. She couldn't quite open her eyes, nor yet raise her head up to breathe.

But she felt the surge of pressure as something rose up from below.

The pulse of her heartbeat, as she saw the rising shadow, was just enough to rouse her, but not enough to move before it was upon her.

This time it was the big female matriarch – Bonnie Parker – that came up beneath her.

As she clung to the massive female's fin, she was aware of the rest of the pod, racing past.

Doby crested again, and Lauren saw him bleeding from fresh wounds on his tail-flukes.

Behind them, the rest of the pod had separated the adolescents.

Bonnie turned away from the pursuit, and with Lauren mounted on her back, she circled back to where Tommy had been attempting to follow in *The Argonaut*.

As Bonnie passed below the rear deck, she reared-up in the water. Lauren felt herself snatched off the orca-mama's back like a hawk grabbing a rabbit, and then she was standing on-board.

Cody had her by the arm.

She stared back at him, shivering, dripping-wet and wide-eyed.

"Now THAT," Cody said, "was some crazy shit."

He regarded her with a healthy new respect.

At a momentary loss for words, Lauren couldn't even respond it had been *completely* involuntary.

She choked, spitting salt-water.

Doby breached yet again, this time attempting to land on top of his smaller pursuers.

But at long last, it looked as if the big cachalot was finally beginning to tire.

He couldn't dive deep – the orcas would steal his air. He couldn't ride the surface – they pummeled his gut and severed his fins.

All that was left was to fight.

With Lauren now on-board, Tommy wasted no more time, turning away from the fray.

The two arriving choppers were currently evacuating the last of the remaining survivors off the backs of the floating whales.

The tug-mate was the last to board.

And now, approaching from the north, was what looked like a Navy vessel.

The rescue was pulling out the big guns.

Although, as survivors went, they were already pretty much cleared out. What was left, was the wreckage.

That, and Doby's final stand.

Cody tossed a towel over Lauren's shivering shoulders as they watched the bedeviled leviathan, battling back against his tormentors.

But now they were beginning to force his head beneath the surface.

And this time, when the mighty bull did not immediately burst back in a powerful breech, the tailing adolescents lost their nerve.

The first of them broke away, attempting to elude pursuit, but the orcas simply split off, continuing to maul and harass. The smallest of the three, and now by himself, the turncoat, quickly succumbed to the relentless pressure, was dragged underwater and drowned. The forty-five-foot body went limp as the orcas moved in, working together to tear out its tongue.

Below the surface, the off-shore pods were systematically culling the sharks.

Lauren had seen orcas do similar things with mackerel and tuna, large fish in their own right, corralling them into each other, getting them to fight and bite at each other – then moving in to tear them apart.

Doby fought to the last. And the orcas took their lumps.

Ahab took a slashing bite from the cachalot's fourteen-foot jaw, leaving racking wounds nearly the full-length of his body. Orky was already sporting several shark-bites – one over his white patch, leaving a ghastly red gouge. He survived the fight with Doby only after nearly getting his skull crushed by a smashing tail.

But eventually, Doby's struggles ended too.

They were maybe two-hundred yards out when the big cachalot was finally forced beneath the surface for the final time.

The orcas continued to punish his sinking body – in the case of Doby, they were making absolutely sure.

Then they started tearing at his jaw, ripping out his tongue.

Tommy's radio blared, as the Navy vessel drew near – curt instructions to vacate the area, and to report to authorities on shore.

"Heard that before," Cody muttered. But he gave Lauren's shivering shoulder a squeeze.

Lauren looked out at the floating wrecks, the choppers hovering overhead, loaded with the last of the survivors – whose numbers now included her.

"You know," she said quietly, "I'd really like to get the hell out of here."

Tommy nodded. "I hear that."

The orca pods had pulled back, circling, seeming to wait as the Navy vessel pulled close.

Then, as if handing-off the situation, satisfied sufficient human-back-up had arrived, the orcas sounded and disappeared.

Both the transients and the off-shore pods vanished together.

The surviving rogues lingered a while longer.

Orphan Annie was dead. Sometime during the struggle, the Skipper had joined her. Their bodies floated lifelessly, next to what remained of the dead baleens.

So far, their bodies remained unmolested by any sharks – those that survived had fled, those that hadn't sank to the bottom. Many of these dead sharks' butchered carcasses would wash ashore the next day. Several would be found with human remains inside.

Lauren looked back as *The Argonaut* pulled away.

She saw the fins of the rogue pod, headed off to sea.

Corky tarried on the perimeter. Pete said she was always the last one out after curfew, last in the pen at night, the last out of the bay.

For a moment, Corky spy-hopped.

Pete stepped up to the railing, as if catching her eye.

Then with a final splash, Corky sounded and was gone.

CHAPTER 40

Once the Navy arrived, the clean-up was short and sweet. The wrecked boats were cleared out by the end of the day. None had sunk all the way to the bottom, so the wreckage could mostly be towed.

They also took care of what was left of the whale carcasses, separating them, towing them out to sea, and then detonating them.

Survivors were taken to shore.

All that was left was to tally up the dead.

It would take time to reach an accurate count. The press maintained a daily update as the toll mounted over the following days.

As it turned out, the live-feed maintained through the entire event. Cameras attached to both the wrecked boats and the tethered whales remained active.

It had been Kate Foster who had leased the feed, and because she had not done so as the member of any group, there was no second-in-command to cancel it.

The whole world watched.

Lacey Chase's final broadcast was already copyrighted, as her network took full-advantage of their exclusive rights.

Liza Carter had gone platinum. Her brief film career – approximately six made-for-cable movies, along with TV show guest-spots – was now lionized on DVDs that couldn't be kept in stock. As the press ran with the story, Liza Carter became its celebrity face, and was currently as famous as any *living* actress in her immediate generation.

The press was actually stuck on how to treat the story – uncertain whether to focus on the human tragedy, or perhaps the ecological implications – or possibly even the criminal aspects.

As it played out, human nature dictated most of those decisions.

The ecologists, for example, were not in a position to judge. For all their officialdom, the high-brow institutions *and* the high-minded activist groups had given their stamp. And at this point, rather than complaining about the damage to ecology – for example, the brief, reflexive objection after the Navy's use of munitions – most of those in official positions were checking on their legal liabilities regarding the dead and injured.

Mayor Kirby of North Shore was on TV, promising serious scrutiny of the tragedy, and prompt accountability. *If* justified.

But a lot of that was side-stepped, at least in the short-term, as Judge Michelle Rosin, after consultation with the local DA's office, announced that no criminal charges would be pursued by the city.

She also ruled that any proceeds from the production be put towards damages.

That was a favorable ruling, because as it turned out, there were a LOT of proceeds.

The live-stream broadcast had gone global – a pay-per-view click on every order.

Yes, the tragedy was shaping up as a real windfall.

Of course, there was still that pesky detail of accountability.

A lot of people had died.

It defied propriety that no one be blamed.

CHAPTER 41

Kate was checking out of her hotel. One way or another, it would probably be the last dive she would ever stay in for the rest of her life.

Odds were, going forward, she would now have her *own* money, or a prison cell.

Maybe both. How fast she got the first, had a lot to do with the second.

In the days since the disaster, she had been 'asked' by the city, with encouragement from the state, that she stick around the area – 'just until we get everything sorted out.'.

Judge Rosin's ruling had streamlined that. And once that was done, public figures could again be seen with her without stigma.

It remained to be seen how the public would judge her. Kate knew very well that bad public perception might influence those in the legal system to find something else on her, just to balance karma – the scales of justice, so-to-speak.

A.G. Walker from Seattle, for example, was one Kate could easily see taking just that sort of advantage.

But around these parts, once the appropriate solemn gestures were made, the bottom-line was that Kate had delivered.

The disaster was not her fault. The involvement of the rogue whale could not possibly have been foreseen. More than reasonable safety precautions *had* been taken.

There were those who would try to blame her anyway – and more importantly, *sue* her, simply for staging the event – but negligence was not the cause of any deaths.

And Kate always covered her bases.

It showed in the little things – like arranging so only *she* could cut the live-feed.

She *could* have at any time – she'd lost *her* phone, but could have used Lauren's. Not that she'd thrown that little fact on the record.

Kate had delivered the product – and the show, as it were, had indeed exceeded the hype.

In the immediate future, it would be edited, packaged, and available for purchase on DVD, live-stream, pay-per-view.

The numbers she'd seen on the early-estimates were humbling.

Still, it was likely the incident would hurt her in the hard-core, purist sector of the conservationist community.

How had Lauren described it? Nauseatingly exploitive?

Miss bare-ass had said that.

Her precious Institute was looking at potential lawsuits too, but because of Kate, those lawsuits, *and* their lawyers, would be paid.

Asked if it was worth the lives, she would have said *no*.

But they did earn a *lot* of money.

The docudrama was recast, and already filmed – in a studio tank on a sound stage, using animatronic sharks, recycled and repainted from at least three different low-budget 'killer-shark' flicks. It was done, cut, and released, before it could be legally blocked – and then it was released again, spliced with live-footage of the actual incident itself.

Lauren – who Kate was back to calling *Doctor Palmer* – had winced at the thought. She had, however, made no comment nor any attempt to withhold her signature from the appropriate forms, not blocking the proceedings in any way.

She was acting head of the Institute now.

After all, she'd been 'promoted'. She had the sharks to thank for *that*.

And now that the office was hers, Lauren was willing enough to accept the higher-budget.

It was also possible she'd learned to stay out of Kate's way.

Or, she thought, eyeing Doctor Palmer over her desk, was it possible she might still intend to hamstring her later?

Kate's eyes narrowed.

"We're friends, right?" she asked. "Going forward?"

Lauren had smiled dutifully, sitting back in her chair as Kate rose to leave.

"Let's just say we've got history," she replied.

Kate would take that. Lauren would stay in her little pool. She might bite, if Kate prodded, but there was no need. Cylvia Brown, after all, had given the Institute's official stamp. It was on the record and done.

That left one loose, dangling string.

And there he was, checking out of the same motel, having now been released from his own travel-restriction by Judge Rosin's ruling.

Pete tapped his cane on the wooden walkway – putting his weight almost normally on his wounded leg, Kate noted.

He held up a small pack and nodded to the cab waiting in the parking lot.

"Still going in style," he said. "You know, I think I'm the only one that didn't make money on this deal."

He shrugged, hefting his pack. "The only one that lived, anyway."

Kate frowned. Cheap shot.

Why did he have to *do* that? What did he want out of her? Guilt? Did he just want her to hurt?

GOD, she thought, he was *infuriating*.

Arrogant. Naive. Stupid.

Idealistic. Unflappable. Courageous, honest – ever-so-slightly chauvinistic.

Just the way you expected a man to *be*.

Kate could read him like a book – every mood swing, every motive.

It was easy – he was the friggin' good-guy.

She knew, for example, that he was blaming himself, at least as much as her.

He had not, after all, called the local DA – or Judge Rosin – *or* Attorney General Walker's office. Now, because he hadn't, he was wondering if it would have made the difference.

Kate knew him well enough to know he was also analyzing his own actions for any hint of selfish motive.

But the honest truth was, while he had certainly expressed safety concerns, even Pete hadn't suspected the full possible extent of the tragedy.

If he had, would he have risked putting Kate – or even himself – in jail to stop it?

Because, if he *had*, there would have been no tragedy to be a hero for stopping – he would simply be a felon.

Personally, Kate thought, *yes*, he probably would have. Had he suspected.

But he hadn't.

What-ifs didn't matter. They all had to live with what *did* happen.

Kate ignored his barb.

"Where are you headed?" she asked.

"Right now? Home. Tommy took the boat back up north a few days ago. He didn't know how long I'd be stuck in town." He checked his watch. "I'm headed for the bus depot."

"I mean, what are your plans?"

He sighed. "Well, I wanted to get back out on the water. But..."

Now, his normally wry, amiable face seemed to wither, looking his age for the first time since she'd known him.

"Honestly," he said. "I'm just too damned tired."

His eyes cut regretfully towards the ocean as he spoke.

Kate nodded, understanding.

"You want to know what happened to them, don't you?" she said. "I saw one..."

"The Skipper," Pete said, quickly. "And Annie. Both got hit."

He shut his eyes, not wanting to dwell, looking forward instead.

"Tommy said he saw Corky and the others heading off with the transients."

"You think they'll take her?" Kate asked.

Pete looked at her in that way of his, oddly personal, even penetrating – because this was something unique they had between them.

"I don't know," he said. "I hope so. But it's never happened before."

He left the rest unsaid – there were a lot of things, just lately, that had never happened before.

Now he leaned forward on his cane so he could look in her eyes.

"What about you, Kate?" he asked. "How much trouble are you in?"

Kate eyed him right back.

"That depends a lot on you."

"Well," Pete said, "how about, when AG Walker calls, I testify that the orcas escaped on their own from the facility, that I don't know about any texts to eco-terrorists."

He shrugged. "That would be consistent with my position against releasing them in the first place. And it would absolve you of responsibility, text or no text."

"As the caretaker," Kate said, "it might put it right back on you."

Pete smiled.

"Already thought of that, did you?"

Of course she had.

She also recognized what her mother had called the 'extended-hand'.

Never reach out, she had said. Let them take you by the arm.

Reaching out got your hand grabbed – or chopped off.

"Why?" Kate asked. "Why do that?"

"Beats me," Pete said. "Core optimism? Maybe I have respect for your powers."

He leaned a bit closer.

"I just wish you'd use them for good."

Kate blinked at the insinuation. She stared back challengingly.

"You mean like *you*?"

Pete said nothing, uncertain if she was picking a fight or if she meant it.

In truth, she was picking a fight.

And she meant it.

Because she knew why she had to justify herself to him. It was because he was a good judge of character.

That was why he liked orcas. And not many people.

And he didn't *want* to like *her*.

Yet, here he was, in spite of himself.

Looking at it that way made it even better.

She had his number.

And on that note, she hefted her own bag.

"Well," she said, starting to turn, "my lawyers tell me I'm still not supposed to be around you, so..."

With a wry smile, Pete stepped forward, dispensing with the cane.

When he took her hand, she thought he was going to make a move to kiss her. She wondered if she might let him.

Instead, he curled his hand into her palm and gave it a gentle squeeze and a shake.

He held on just a little longer before he let go.

Kate sighed.

The sonofabitch sure was stingy about his PDA.

Pete hefted his bag, waving to the waiting cab.

"Take care, Kate," he said and turned to leave.

As he left, he nodded to her over his shoulder.

"Be good."

CHAPTER 42

Lauren wondered if she would ever look at the ocean the same way again.

Scratch that. *No* – she never would.

Somewhere in the middle of all the rest, that was a quiet, personal tragedy.

For Lauren, it had always been her place. In a way, it was like falling out of a religious faith. It hurt in ways she hadn't expected.

There was still beauty there. And awe. But it was a terrible beauty.

As was all of nature.

And it left her feeling very small.

Today was her first day back at the Institute – as administrator – and Kate Foster had been in to see her. And speaking of feeling small, Kate had given her the lay-of-the-land, before handing over a big fat paycheck.

Lauren was not like Pete, blaming himself for what he hadn't done – instead, she had done her all, and found it meaningless.

Was that better or worse?

In any case, today, she had simply sat back and let Kate's machinery do its work.

Then Lauren had left the Institute for the day. And instead of going home, she had driven to the beach, kicked off her shoes and started to walk.

It was not too far from The Fish Shack – still the best seafood in town.

She was very aware of what she was doing – walking along the beach, her feet wet from the incoming tide, listening to the soothing roar of the ocean. She was trying to make the magic work again.

But it wasn't the same – like listening to a once-favorite song after a bad break-up. The notes hadn't changed, but the associations were all soured.

That was going to be a problem for her in days ahead – it was how she coped.

She actually wasn't sure what she was going to do.

As it turned out, she was not the only one.

Just up ahead, she saw Cody, sitting on the beach, his pick-up pulled up to the sand, looking out on the ocean.

Lauren paused. She hadn't spoken to him since the day. At the time, they had been pulled apart by officialdom – answering questions, giving statements.

In the days since, she had wanted to call. Specifically because of that, she hadn't.

Now, she debated whether to simply try and slip away.

That was always her way. To play it safe. Carson was always the wild one. Not that Lauren hadn't often been *drawn in...*

Cody, however, turned and caught her eye.

Resigned, Lauren waved. Cody nodded neutrally as she walked up and sat down next to him on the sand.

"Thinking of going surfing?" she asked.

He smiled.

"No," he said.

And by the tone of his voice, Lauren could tell it was different for him too.

The sharks were still there, Lauren knew, and would be back next season. The problem had not gone away because of one gaudy incident. The reality was that Surf Shore was not a safe place anymore.

That meant, of course, that this surf-town no longer had an attraction. Beaches would be closed indefinitely – particularly, now that they understood the full-extent of the danger.

Frankly, Lauren couldn't imagine sanctioning open recreation in the area for the foreseeable future.

On the other hand, it looked like Kate's investment had paid off.

While the live-stream had been panned by anyone who claimed *any* sort of scientific ethic, it had already been click-baited into the millions.

And lest one might worry about monetary liabilities to the families of those that had died, there actually hadn't been that many who'd filed suits, either for damages, or to block production. All of the participants had signed-up for profit-shares – it was to the benefit of their estates to let the production thrive.

In her way, Kate was a genius. The tragedy was going to pay everybody handsomely – even the bereaved. Actual survivors became instant-celebrities. Some were already writing books. The tug-mate had his own website, and seemed to be an item with the waitress-with-the-lower-back-tattoo.

And Surf Shore might not be done as a resort, after all. From what Lauren understood, Mayor Kirby was toying with the idea of shark-tourism.

Lauren couldn't even say the bodies hadn't yet cooled, because most of them had probably been digested.

These and other images were what clouded her mind, as she sat in the cool breeze, looking out at the once-calming ocean.

"It's not the same, is it?" Cody said.

Cody had an odd habit of repeating her thoughts out loud. It probably shouldn't have surprised her. Within their own roles, they had both been Carson's anchor. It was also why they were natural enemies – they both operated in the same niche.

That dynamic, however, had been based on their only link – and Carson was gone.

They knew each other differently now.

"You know what's funny?" Cody said, thoughtfully. "I was just sitting here, and I realized that I have actually got *money* coming."

He cast his eyes sideways, looking for judgment from the privileged sorority girl. But Lauren sat silent, listening.

"*Real* money," Cody said. "Like the sort that I might not have to *worry* about money anymore."

Now his eyes narrowed, skeptically.

"It's not here, yet," he said. "So I don't quite *believe* it. I've been broke so long, it's practically an identity."

Lauren nodded. Another mirrored thought. She actually admired his self-awareness.

"But I figured, I'd just keep being me," he said. "But as I was sitting here, I realized *this* is me."

He spread his hands helplessly out at the ocean.

"But I just don't *want* it, anymore."

He shook his head. "And now I don't really know what to do."

Lauren nodded. She got it.

They sat there for what was actually a pretty nice moment.

Cody sensed it, and quickly broke the spell.

"I see your bikini-videos are going viral again," he said. "Kate put a shot of your bare-ass in a thong on Twitter."

Lauren let her breath out in a slow-burn.

We're friends, Kate had said.

Grrrrr.

Cody pulled up his phone, where he had the image as his background.

"Although," he said, scrolling down the replies, "your fan-base thinks you're *way* hotter than *she* is."

"Yeah," she said indignantly, "like I care about *that*."

And then, muttered under her breath, "Botox bitch."

"Well," Cody said, "to be fair, at one time I thought *you* were a bitch."

Lauren cocked her head. "And now?"

"Well, you're definitely not a *Botox*-bitch."

He looked admiringly down at the image in his hand.

"Look at it this way," he said, "your ass *could* star in a video series."

Cody had an odd way about him. He could piss you off at the same time as turning a remark like that into a sincere compliment.

Besides, Lauren thought, it was *absolutely* true.

And with that she stood, dusting the sand off her famous tush.

"You know what sounds good?" she said.

Lauren nodded to The Fish Shack, just off the pier, less than a mile up the beach.

"Oyster shooters," she said.

Cody laughed, reaching up to let her pull him to his feet.

"I carried Kate out of there last week, now I'm back with you. Annie isn't going to know what to think."

He didn't try to take her hand, or put his arm around her shoulder. Instead, they simply walked in comfortable tandem.

Nature abhors a vacuum, she thought. Whatever second-hand link that had joined them through Carson, also seemed to have crossed their stars.

Resisting it seemed as pointless as pushing back the incoming tide.

"By the way," she said, "thanks for saving my life. Again."

Cody smiled. "You get me next time," he said.

He held up his phone again, where Kate had already posted a new thong-shot.

"Thanks for *this*," he said.

His grin was absolute pure-cheek.

But Lauren smiled back. Because in that moment, as she swatted at his head, grabbing at his phone, she understood what Carson had seen in him – what Cody was good at.

Somehow, he made you *feel* good.

Lauren reached out, taking Cody's arm. He gave a moment of mock-resistance, but allowed her to lean close.

Nature abhors a vacuum.

CHAPTER 43

Bloody Mary crept along near the very bottom of the deepest crevice after the drop-off.

She hadn't yet retreated to the deeper canyons in the open ocean beyond. Like a very old trout, Mary had learned to hunker-down during a ruckus.

Most of the other sharks had fled the area completely. When the off-shore pod had come in, that left a hole going out, and once things started going south, that's where the bulk of them went.

It remained to be seen if they would be back this season, but they certainly would return in the next migration cycle.

The seals, after all, were still there. And most probably, the orcas would be gone.

That was the nice thing about orcas – they liked to be on the move.

Mary heard a few lingering pod-members, pinging along the out-skirts, chasing down any lingering Carcharodons – in orca-parlance, sort of like killing off the last of the keg, Saturday morning after the party.

But eventually, they would grow bored and they would leave.

And once again, Mary would still be there, haunting this beach, taking surfers, the odd kayaker, the way she always had.

And very likely, she always would.

Because there was always that fish you couldn't catch – the one that's learned the hook in the lure.

Dozens of videos showed Mary, brutally hitting seals.

Never decoys. Not once.

And even more than Big Rhonda, who had postured dominance in these waters for all those years, Bloody Mary never missed.

You never saw her coming.

And she always appeared from behind.

Mary cruised slowly, using little energy, keeping close to the bottom, as had always been her way. In the manner that simple animals learned, she had tripped to this strategy long ago, and it had always served her well.

Rules of survival were quite simple.

Whenever possible, stay at the bottom and hide.

And when they weren't looking, swim up and bite them on the ass.

As a life-philosophy, it hadn't failed her yet.

If she were human, the look in her utterly toneless, blank, black eyes might have been smug. Even gleeful.

Perhaps just a touch of arrogance.

Because she didn't see the harlequin-shape coming up from behind.

Corky had learned how to approach sharks. The off-shore pods were deft, and Corky was a fast study.

She hit Bloody Mary hard in the belly just below the gills. And while the big shark was stunned, Corky flipped her over on her back.

Mary's primitive brain clicked into a tonic trance.

Corky's teeth locked on Mary's pectoral fin, and held her still, ticking away the minutes, until she drowned.

When the big orca released her grip, Mary's corpse started to slowly sink.

Corky took a moment to watch as it lazily twisted its way towards the bottom.

Then, off in the distance, she detected a sonar ping.

Insistent.

Bonnie Parker.

Big mama was clicking – and if big sister was going to be running with the transients, she had to do what big mama said.

Something significant in the world had changed.

For whatever reason, Bonnie had broken tradition.

The world had forced it. And the orca would adapt.

Not the least at stake in this deep-sea change, was a bloodline, a transient gene-pool that had remained untainted by outside eco-types since before human prehistory.

Soon, a new calf would be entering Bonnie's pod – a hybrid – and the world would again see something new.

Bonnie pinged again, and now Corky heard Orky clicking urgently, right along.

The kiss-ass didn't want to get in trouble.

Corky chased after Mary's sinking corpse and tore out the liver.

She glanced back in the direction of the waiting pod, still some miles distant.

Orca etiquette was to share. When the off-shore orcas took a shark, the pickings were divided equally. Likewise, when Bonnie's transients took the tongue of a whale.

In a moment of mischievous indulgence, Corky chomped up the liver and devoured the whole thing, even as Mary's eviscerated corpse sank into the gloom.

Then, with a twitch of her tail, and the taste still on her lips, Corky turned and headed back out to sea.

She was pretty sure Bonnie and the others wouldn't be too upset. Transients didn't like shark anyway.

And after all, she was eating for two.

THE END

CHECK OUT OTHER GREAT DEEP SEA THRILLERS

SEA RAPTOR
by John J. Rust

From terrorist hunter to monster hunter! Jack Rastun was a decorated U.S. Army Ranger, until an unfortunate incident forced him out of the service. He is soon hired by the Foundation for Undocumented Biological Investigation and given a new mission, to search for cryptids, creatures whose existence has not been proven by mainstream science. Teaming up with the daring and beautiful wildlife photographer Karen Thatcher, they must stop a sea monster's deadly rampage along the Jersey Shore. But that's not the only danger Rastun faces. A group of murderous animal smugglers also want the creature. Rastun must utilize every skill learned from years of fighting, otherwise, his first mission for the FUBI might very well be his last.

OCEAN'S HAMMER
by D.J. Goodman

Something strange is happening in the Sea of Cortez. Whales are beaching for no apparent reason and the local hammerhead shark population, previously believed to be fished to extinction, has suddenly reappeared. Marine biologists Maria Quintero and Kevin Hoyt have come to investigate with a television producer in tow, hoping to get footage that will land them a reality TV show. The plan is to have a stand-off against a notorious illegal shark-fishing captain and then go home.

Things are not going according to plan.

There is something new in the waters of the Sea of Cortez. Something smart. Something huge. Something that has its own plans for Quintero and Hoyt.

CHECK OUT OTHER GREAT
DEEP SEA THRILLERS

MEGA
by Jake Bible

There is something in the deep. Something large. Something hungry. Something prehistoric.
And Team Grendel must find it, fight it, and kill it.
Kinsey Thorne, the first female US Navy SEAL candidate has hit rock bottom. Having washed out of the Navy, she turned to every drink and drug she could get her hands on. Until her father and cousins, all ex-Navy SEALS themselves, offer her a way back into the life: as part of a private, elite combat Team being put together to find and hunt down an impossible monster in the Indian Ocean. Kinsey has a second chance, but can she live through it?

THE BLACK
by Paul E Cooley

Under 30,000 feet of water, the exploration rig Leaguer has discovered an oil field larger than Saudi Arabia, with oil so sweet and pure, nations would go to war for the rights to it. But as the team starts drilling exploration well after exploration well in their race to claim the sweet crude, a deep rumbling beneath the ocean floor shakes them all to their core. Something has been living in the oil and it's about to give birth to the greatest threat humanity has ever seen.

"The Black" is a techno/horror-thriller that puts the horror and action of movies such as Leviathan and The Thing right into readers' hands. Ocean exploration will never be the same."

CHECK OUT OTHER GREAT DEEP SEA THRILLERS

MEGATOOTH
by Viktor Zarkov

When the death rate of sperm whales rises dramatically, a well-respected environmental activist puts together a ragtag team to hit the high seas to investigate the matter. They suspect that the deaths are due to poachers and they are all driven by a need for justice.

Elsewhere, an experimental government vessel is enhancing deep sea mining equipment. They see one of these dead whales up close and personal...and are fairly certain that it wasn't poachers that killed it.

Both of these teams are about to discover that poachers are the least of their worries. There is something hunting the whales...

Something big
Something prehistoric.
Something terrifying.
MEGATOOTH!

BLOOD CRUISE
by Jake Bible

Ben Clow's plans are set. Drop off kids, pick up girlfriend, head to the marina, and hop on best friend's cruiser for a weekend of fun at sea. But Ben's happy plans are about to be changed by a tentacled horror that lurks beneath the waves.

International crime lords! Deep cover black ops agents! A ravenous, bloodsucking monster! A storm of evil and danger conspire to turn Ben Clow's vacation from a fun ocean getaway into a nightmare of a Blood Cruise!